I0619890

FESTUM MORS

C.A. RENE

THE ENIGMA SOCIETY

INSIDIOUS

BY SUKI WILLIAMS

DISSEVER

BY ALLY VANCE

DELETERIOUS

BY YOLANDA OLSON

FESTUM MORS

BY C.A. RENE

NEVERMORE

BY SIAN B. CLAVEN

COME HITHER, DARK DREAMER

BY DEE GARCIA

ROMANCE IS DEAD

BY TAMSYN BESTER AND ROBIN ASH

DANCING ON GRAVES

BY JORDAIN KNOLLS

IMMOLATION

BY EMERY LEEANN

Copyright Festum Mors © 2022 C.A. Rene

All rights reserved. This book, or any portion thereof, may not be reproduced or used in any manner whatsoever without the express written permission of the publisher, except for the use of brief quotations in a book review.

This book is a work of fiction, and any resemblance to any person, living or dead, is purely coincidental. The characters and storylines are created by the author's imagination and are used fictitiously.

No copyright infringement intended.

Cover Design by; Jay Aheer @ Simply defined Art

Formatting by:

Paperback ISBN: 978-1-990675-11-9

CONTENT WARNING

This is a dark MM retelling of The Cask of Amontillado by Edgar Allan Poe

This story contains scenes of graphic sexual content. Alcohol consumption and the use of drugs to incapacitate. There is a graphic scene of murder. Please read with discretion.

PROLOGUE

The wine splashes from the mouth of the bottle as I let it slip from my fingers, hitting the ground with a *thud*. The cellar is cold, damp, and dark, a perfect description of my heart.

It's been a week since I built a wall, encasing my heart, and sealing it away forever. One entire week of crying and screaming, of hating myself, but never once changing my mind.

My suit, once a pristine cream color, is now wrinkled, the material coated in the dust and filth of the cellar. I've been wearing it for nearly seven days. The opulent silk attire was chosen by my sister for her grand wedding, a true societal affair.

The day everything changed.

My body aches from sleeping on the floor, inside a room which smells of urine and vomit, a mix so nauseating I retch into the dark. Still, I can't find a single regret.

I torture myself for the mistakes I've made, for the promises I failed to keep, and the families I've ruined. That's why this promise can never be broken. It's encased behind stone and mortar, never to be discovered.

The heart may be fickle, but true love can never die.

2 MONTHS EARLIER

I step out onto my bedroom's balcony to watch the sun set in fantastical shades of reds and oranges. Nothing beats Italy's sunrise or sunset. There is simply no comparison.

The breeze filters in, picking up my curly black hair and kissing the nape of my neck. A chill courses down my spine, raising goosebumps along my skin. Something ominous is in the air. I can feel it.

"Monty!"

I lean over the stone balustrade to find my best friend Ford waving his hands.

"Come on down, Monty! We are riding the canal tonight."

I straighten up with a groan. I'm tired of the same gondola rides along the canal. It's all becoming so boring. Ford and I are past the childish ages of running through the Venetian streets and causing havoc. We should be looking to our futures, planning the rest of our lives.

I am bored.

"Monty!" he hollers again. "Diana and Christina will be there."

He thinks he's enticing me by telling me two of the most beautiful girls will be riding with us, and maybe if this was a month ago, I would be swayed. Right now, it's all mundane.

"Come inside, Ford."

I hear the front door open as I head back inside my bedroom, the sound echoing around my cavernous home. My parents are Diplomats and are rarely here, and my sister is a free spirit who loves to go wherever her heart takes her. Danielle is older than me by two years, and she hasn't been home since her twentieth birthday three months ago.

I practically live alone.

Luckily for me, my parents are wine connoisseurs and crates of imported fine wine are shipped here regularly. So on the days I'm feeling like this, I find a crate of their very best wine, and I help myself to a bottle or two.

Tonight I decided to open the crate of amontillado. I've already helped myself to nearly a full bottle, and when Ford and I come face-to-face, me at the top of the stairs and him at the bottom, his eyes slide up with glee.

"Monty, have you been dipping into the good stuff?"

"Not just the good stuff, my friend." I sway a little on the spot as I grab the banister for stability. "The best my parents have in the cellar."

"I don't know how you pull it off," he chuckles. "How do they not notice that their wine is missing when they come home?"

"Because, Ford," I tsk as I start to descend the stairs. "They don't give a fuck about me, and as long as I'm not bothering them, I could drink myself to death for all they care."

"I need to try this wine," he says. "Only I can judge if this is an excellent wine."

Ford has convinced himself that this past summer he's become an expert in wine. He began dating Christina whose family owns a vineyard, and I say dating loosely because Ford has never committed himself to her per se, but he sure likes her family money and the free wine.

Probably something he enjoys about being my friend too, and I would question him for it if we hadn't been friends since we were seven years old.

"I'll let you have some of this wine," I tell him as I reach the bottom of the stairs, my hand landing on his shoulder, giving it a gentle squeeze. "If you end up throwing up this very expensive wine, you will owe me something."

"I don't throw up," he scoffs. "You're on, but, Monty," he counters as he follows me into my kitchen. "You will owe me something if I don't throw up."

"Sounds fair." I shrug. "What is it you want?"

"You will begin to be the perfect wingman when I need you to be. When Christina brings Diana on our dates, you must come without a single complaint."

I roll my eyes at the juvenile favor, but I let it go. I'm not too worried because I know Ford cannot handle this wine, and I give it one bottle before he's throwing up.

"Fine," I agree.

"Yes!" His fist hits the countertop. "Now tell me, even though it's unnecessary because I will not lose, what will I owe you?"

His earnest brown eyes meet mine as his full lips tip up into a mischievous smirk. I give him a slow once-over, finding myself slightly surprised with his outfit tonight.

He's wearing cream linen trousers with a white shirt, the top three buttons open, revealing the newly grown hair on his chest. His skin is a deep olive, setting off the vibrancy of the white, and his slicked back dark hair shines with a pomade under my kitchen lights.

"I'm not sure yet." I shrug. "But like you said, it doesn't matter, right?"

"Exactly." He snaps his fingers. "It's really unnecessary." His face is lit up, the thrill of having a wager on the table ramping up our excitement.

We've been doing this since we were kids. A game of dare and enticement. The wagers have always been small, nothing we couldn't fulfill in the end.

It's proof to the fact that I've literally been bored my entire life.

I wave for Ford to follow me to the cellar, a place he's always been wary of. In his defense, it's dark, it's gloomy, and there's a chill that penetrates to your very bones. But unfortunately, it's necessary because I have already finished the bottle I brought upstairs earlier.

"I hate this place," he mutters as we descend stairs. The concrete under our feet echoes with each footfall, the sound bouncing off the stone walls and amplifying the creepiness of the underground vault.

Almost like a labyrinth of corridors, a feature that really sold my parents on this place. They love the fact that we have our very own mini catacombs under our house.

I lead him to the open crate, pushing aside the straw encasing the bottles and yanking two out. As I turn to look at him, I hand him one. I can see the fear in his dark eyes, the way his teeth sink into his plush bottom lip.

"Come on, baby," I snicker at him as I shove him back toward the stairs. "We should make another bet, in case you shit your pants."

"Fuck you, Monty." He shakes his head.

FORD

Monty is a rich snob. His house is ostentatious, his bank account knows no limit, and his parents forget he exists. I envy him for all of it.

We step out of the creepy cellar, and he gives me another once-over, chuckling with whatever it is he sees on my face. I don't care if the place freaks me out, and I don't care how funny he finds it. I'm not looking to die when those crumbling walls cave in.

As he walks ahead of me, I take in his appearance. His silk shirt moves like liquid, and I bet if I pinched it between my fingers, the black fabric would feel like butter. He has the sleeves rolled up around his elbows, showing off his toned and tanned forearms. I envy him that, too.

Monty Marcato has all the time in the world to pump weights and jog around town. He doesn't have a day job to worry about. Would it be redundant if I said I envied him again?

I have to work two jobs to maintain my schooling, and to keep up with the lifestyle my rich best friend prefers.

I know I sound like I'm complaining, but despite all of these envious feelings I have, I do enjoy being his best friend. We've known each other for too long, and even though I want to wrap my hands around his throat most days, I love him as well.

"Are those silk pajamas?" I ask as I snicker at the matching silk pants.

"They are well above what you can afford," he grins at me over his shoulder. "I'll let you borrow them after I fuck Christina. Silk holds scent so well."

"Christina thinks you're an arrogant bastard," I chuckle. "She would never spread her legs for you."

"She enjoys slumming it, hm?"

Monty has a deep voice, the low tenor holding a raspy edge. Coupled with his good looks and net value, it's surprising how he rarely dates. He's picky, I know that, and he's insecure about being used, something I don't understand, but I feel like there's something more.

Christina DiFonso's family is not as rich as the Marcatos, but they have more than they'll ever be able to spend in this lifetime. So, when he says she's slumming it with me, he's not lying. It's her bit of rebellion before her parents force her to settle down, while my own are hoping it's with me.

It won't be.

Hence why I don't get too attached. I would hate to find myself head over heels, only to lose her to another. It's much better if I play my games and guard my heart.

Monty tosses me his signature lopsided grin as he pulls out two wine glasses. I watch his arms flex as he pops the cork, his dark skin rippling with the motion. He spends most of his time smoking on his bedroom balcony, the sun toasting his skin into a deep olive. It makes his striking blue eyes pop out from his otherwise average face.

His nose is a little too big, his mouth turned downward, and his facial hair a little too sporadic, but those eyes are a Marcato gene. His father and sister have the same ones.

Envious, you may wonder?

Why, yes. Yes, I am.

"Now, Ford," he smirks as the dark red sherry fills the glass. "Let's have a toast."

My long fingers wrap around the thin stem of the wine glass, my nail beds still stained with grease from the garage I work in. No matter how much I scrape and scrub, they are never quite as pristine as Monty's.

"What shall we toast to?" I ask him. "I'm genuinely curious. What could it be that Monty would deem toast-worthy?"

"Let's toast to our friendship. You, Ford, are my very best friend, and tonight we are going to test your so-called iron stomach."

His words send tendrils of shame throughout my stomach, the feeling casting my heart in guilt. Monty cares about me, and even though he likes to poke fun at me, I know he would do anything for me.

"To our friendship." I nod as I hold up my glass, his eyes narrow and those icy blues slowly slip along my face and down to the wine glass suspended in the air. When his clanks against the rim of mine, the sound breaks the hold of his eyes, and we both tip our heads back and down the first class in one swallow.

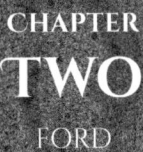

My head pounds with a rhythm only my stomach can resonate with. I slowly peel my tongue off the roof of my mouth, the feeling sending shards of painful tingles throughout my palette. My nostrils flare as I take in a long, deep breath, the surrounding air tinged with a faint scent of vomit.

I groan as I slowly turn, knowing my upper lip is probably coated with my stomach's acid, and as the movement sends my world on its axis, I've realized I've lost our bet.

When I crack open my eyes, the lids slowly peeling apart, my vision is obscured by a thin film of mucus. No matter how unfocused the room is before me, I see the outline of the opulent mantle. Its surface covered in thick Italian marble, the veins of gold glittering throughout, stands clear. I am still at Monty Marcato's house. I just don't know what happened after the sixth glass of wine.

The taste of bile mixed with what seems to be nicotine dances along the surface of my tongue as I slowly swallow down the thick saliva that's pooled inside my mouth. If I had a cigarette last night, it means I had long passed my limit, and as always, nicotine amplifies my hangovers.

I slowly sit up on the stiff couch, the cushions feeling similar to stone slabs, and my neck pulsing with pain. At least I had a blanket wrapped around what looks to be my very naked body, and I find my clothing folded on the table in front of me.

Being naked doesn't surprise me. I sleep in the nude, and I would assume it was my last conscious thought to remove the hindrance of fabric before slumber overtook me. But it was the kindness of my best friend to fold one of my best outfits.

My bladder screams for release as I stand and grab my boxers from the stack of clothing. I drag them on, taking my time to slip each foot into the hole. I'm praying my stomach calms down.

With each footfall, my toes curl into the plush carpet of the sitting room. But as soon as I hit the corridor, a welcome chill from the marble-tiled floor slips up through my heated body, eliciting a moan of pleasure from my mouth. It's short lived when I hear an arrogant snicker sound from behind me.

I turn to look over my shoulder and find Monty with his arms crossed over his bare chest, his skin an even dark bronze, telling me he's often shirtless on his balcony. His lips curve up into a taunting grin as his frigid eyes scan me over from head to toe in a long, scrutinizing look.

"Ford," he tsks. "I think you lost a bet."

"Monty," I moan, the sound of his name rolling off my tongue like a forbidden secret. "I fucking know I did."

His laugh is deep and raspy as I turn away and continue my travels toward the bathroom.

"I'll get you some food," he calls out.

I step into the bathroom, foregoing the lights, knowing the bright fluorescence of the vanity would only refract in agonizing fractions of light. My head and my stomach just couldn't handle it this early in the day.

I leave the bathroom feeling much lighter, even so, the throbbing in my head feels like an intense summer storm. The kind that possesses aggressive thunder that shakes the foundation of your home.

The scent of scallions and butter, mixed with eggs and seasoning, hit me full force as I round the corner into the kitchen. My mouth waters at the same time as my stomach flips. I'm hungry, but I'm fucking ill.

"That wine, it was tainted," I groan as I slip into the cushion stool at the large island that takes up a mere fraction of the expansive kitchen.

"It was not," he chuckles. "It was just too rich for your stomach."

"A double entendre." I fall forward onto the stone island top and let the cool surface seep through my flaming face. "Were you not affected at all?"

"I was inebriated," he confirms. "But I have quite the tolerance."

"That's because you have all the time in the day to drink as much as you want," I groan as a plate is placed in front of me.

"That is true."

And there it is, the envy that never fully leaves me when I'm in Monty's presence. There's very little reprieve from the annoying feeling. Even during the moments when I feel like I'm dancing on death's doorsteps.

"I have work today," I whine.

"At the shop?" His head tips to the side.

"No, the carnival is back in town, and this year, they're paying double what the garage does per hour."

"What are you going to be? A carny? Are you serious?"

He has that arrogant smirk on his face. As if I have a choice but to work, as if I could afford to turn down a position that would give me thousands of dollars in the month that it's here.

"It looks like it." I snatch the fork from his offered hand and let the metal prongs clank loudly from the ceramic surface of the plate.

Who am I kidding? This is probably fine china I'm eating off of.

"Don't be mad, Ford." Monty's hand grips my arm, halting the fork just as it's about to hit my lips. "I was just playing around. I think it's cool you're going to be working at the carnival. Maybe I'll stop by."

It's hard to decipher if he's being genuine or not. Not that I have the brain cells to use toward such an arduous task right now. He releases my forearm, and I shovel eggs into my mouth, moaning as the buttery texture melts on top of my tongue.

"I'm never drinking again." My lips work the words out around a mouth full of eggs.

"You say this every time," he chuckles.

"What are you going to do today?" I ask him, halting just before I was about to add *while I work my ass off.* I don't want to fan the flames. It'll only leave us scorched in an inferno.

"Probably work out a bit." He shrugs. "Same thing I do every day."

My spine straightens as I hear hints of disdain in his voice. The words don't sound like they're coming from the mouth of a satisfied person. He sounds bored.

"Maybe you should get a job at the carnival too," I suggest.

"Only if I get to wear one of those jester hats." He tosses me a wink.

There's always one fool at the carnival each year who dons a fool's outfit with the jester hat to match.

MONTY

The heels of my shoes click against the cobble-stone walkway as I head toward the sounds of laughter and cheer.

After Ford left my house this morning, grumbling about having to work at the carnival, I did my workout, which helped sweat out the hangover I too was suffering from. Then I forced myself to get dressed and leave the house.

I know I'm harsh on him and sometimes the things that come out of my mouth aren't well thought out verbiage, but he's tolerated me for years and he doesn't always deserve the vitriol I spit. My parents deserve it. Hell, even my sister deserves it, but not Ford.

I know he looks at my lifestyle, at my material possessions, and wishes we could exchange places. And even though I would never admit this to him, there are days—and lately they're becoming more frequent—that I wish we could switch as well.

He has a family who takes care of him. A mother and father who adore their only child, he has a warm plate of food in front of him each evening, and an unconditional love he doesn't realize can be so rare.

"Monty!"

Diana Federico's high-pitched squeal interrupts my wholesome musings, and I stop in my tracks to wait as the sounds of her heels bounce off the cobblestones, growing nearer.

Her hand slips around my forearm as she comes to stand beside me and I give it a sharp shrug, discarding the offending appendage.

Few people are allowed to touch me, and Diana is not one of them. Besides, her touch sands a sensation along my skin like scrambling cockroaches. I pull my smokes out of my pocket, bringing one to my mouth as she stands there watching me, her mouth moving with irritation in my peripheral vision. I slowly bring my lighter to the tip, taking a long drag and slowly watching as the cherry brightens. I inhale the acrid smoke, and then finally turn to face the annoying female, exhaling it in a plume of chemicals around her face.

She begins to frantically wave her hand back and forth, letting a fake chuckle escape through her red painted lips. Finally, I give her a scrutinizing once-over and see she's wearing a thin yellow sundress, the color making her dark olive skin pop. Her hair is twisted up into a bun on top of her head with curls escaping the tight confines. It looks like maybe she's highlighted her usual brown hair, but I can't be sure. Those eyes look up at me, slightly moist from the attack of smoke, making her brown irises shine with the slightest hint of honey.

"Are you going to the carnival?" Her head tips to the side, elongating her thin neck and showcasing the pulsing vein just under the skin.

I take another long drag of my cigarette as my eyes dip down past her collarbone to take in her ample chest and the very evident fact that she is not wearing a bra. Her nipples began to tighten under my scrutinizing, and I can just imagine her brown areolas begging for my mouth's attention.

"Possibly," I answer as the smoke escapes from my nose and mouth.

"Ford is there, and Christina and I are playing a game."

My ears perk up at the sound of a game. I do love a distraction. "What game?"

"We need to find Ford and see what position he's been given. He's been quiet about it, and he said the only way we can find out is if we go there and see for ourselves."

Her voice is too high-pitched, the screeching tenor only heightening under certain lilts and syllables, making my teeth gnash together with irritation. Her excitement is palpable, and it takes everything in me not to snort in her face.

"Will you join us?" Her right hand slips up to touch her collarbone, the tips of her nails painted in a blood red to match her lips, and I bet to any other warm-blooded male she'd be tantalizing, but to me, she looks like a clown.

"Why not?" I say as I flick my cigarette to the side of the road.

I begin to walk forward, my strides double hers, ensuring I stay well ahead of the cloying scent of her perfume. It's something like oranges and vanilla, teetering on the edge of rot. It makes my stomach roll, threatening to toss up the half a bottle of amontillado I've already consumed. I should have drank the whole fucking thing. Maybe it would have been easier to approach this situation with dulled senses.

"Christina's house is on the way. I told her I'd meet her there." Diana keeps talking, and I know where Christina's house is. Her family owns one of the largest vineyards in Venice. Therefore, she lives close to me.

I continue toward the sounds of the carnival, the tinkling music filling the night air, and the sounds of the MCS as they try to coerce the patrons to play their games.

Just as the air is taking on the scent I love, sugary treats and decadent BBQ, Christina's house appears to the left, and there she is, standing at the edge of the driveway with a more demure dress hanging from her shoulders. The white lace tells of an innocent woman, and her slender frame gives off more of a child-like essence, nothing like her voluptuous friend at my side.

Her makeup-free face blooms with happiness at the sight of Diana, who once again squeals with a frequency I'm sure only a dog can appreciate. As they rush toward each other, the sounds of their heels bouncing off the cobblestones are like a cacophony of knives sinking into my skull. They embrace in a wave of siren calls as I continue walking straight ahead and right past them.

"Monty Marcato?" Christina's curious voice hits the back of my head. "Will you be joining us this evening?" At least her voice is a tolerable tone, not one that fractures glass.

"I think it's more like we're headed in the same direction," I call over my shoulder without breaking my stride.

"It really is a full moon tonight." She laughs, the raspy sound traveling to the appendage between my legs. It begins to thicken as I contemplate what exactly that could mean. Do I want Christina because she looks a little purer? Or is it because she is attached to Ford?

I give a shrug of my shoulders, answering both her and myself in one swift motion.

They follow behind me, staying a few paces back, their whispering voices tangling with the sounds of the approaching carnival. I must admit, breathing in the fresh air from my balcony in comparison to the fresh air in the middle of the town is quite different. I feel more invigorated, and something akin to excitement swirls in my stomach.

My eyes skim along the star-filled sky and land on what is indeed a bright full moon.

It reminds me of stories, of myths told. How our inner monsters break from our skin to enjoy the full moon, how our baser instincts override our intellectual thought, creating chaos all under the glowing orb.

Maybe that's what's stirring deep inside me. My inner monster is answering the call of the full moon, readying to tear through my skin and have its one night of freedom.

"Monty!" Christina calls out. "Where do you think we'll find Ford?"

"My first guess would be the kissing booth."

Their collective gasps have my mouth flipping upward into a smirk. Ford could very well be at the kissing booth. He refuses to commit completely to Christina, and she knows it.

"He wouldn't." Diana's voice grates on my last frayed nerve. "He wouldn't dare."

"You're dating him." I turn to look at Christina, her features riddled with worry, telling me she is more invested in Ford than I suspected. "Would he dare?"

"I don't own him." Her chin lifts with a sign of defiance. "He can do what he wants."

I shrug again as the large, checkered-pattern tents begin to rise in front of us. The neon colors light up the sky in a magnificent technicolor display. Music pours from the speakers and voices scream into mics, enticing people to try their food or play their games.

My heart picks up its rhythm as my eyes scan the scene in front of me. So many people are laughing and joking, and right there in the center of the carnival, standing on a podium, is none other than the jester himself. He's dressed in a jumpsuit of patchwork patterns, bright colors competing with the neon lights. His face is painted in great detail of the comedy mask, the eerie, wide grin sending chills down my spine.

He swings a baton in front of him, the ends lit with fire. As soon as his arm lifts and he swings it over his head, I see those fingers with the nails lightly lined with faded grease. My mouth stretches into a smile that would compete with the one painted on his face.

Ford fumbles the baton, nearly catching two people on fire as it drops to the ground. His hands steeple under his chin as his head tips to the side in a look of apology, all the while everyone laughs at his antics.

His eyes scan the crowd, and then they land on me as I slowly approach him, staying wide with glee.

Not for the first time I wish my life were as care-free as Ford's.

THREE

MONTY

The girls scamper off toward the kissing booth, none the wiser of who is beneath the jester's outfit. Not even Christina, who swears she knows Ford better than anyone else, but yet, here I am standing in front of him with my arms crossed.

I found him within sixty seconds of entering the carnival.

He continues to dance on the podium, his legs flinging out, and those ridiculous bells jingling from his hat with the movement. Everyone gathered around roars with appreciation, and I feel my own admiration rise. Ford is like a jack of all trades. He grasps everything that's thrown in front of him and learns to roll with it, then he masters it.

I respect that about him.

Finally, he drops this small banjo down to the podium, and begins to step down to a chorus of boos. The crowd wants him to keep going, to entertain them, but when those painted eyes meet mine, I see the exhaustion in their depths.

The crowd disperses as I grab Ford's arm and yank him toward the back of the nearest tent. The colorful fabric effectively blocks out any of the neon lights, and both of us are shrouded in shadows.

"How did you know it was me?" he asks, his voice sounding weary but that face still ridiculously happy. Such a distinct contrast.

This would have been where I told him the truth if I were feeling like myself. I would tell him it was the grime that's embedded in his nails, the nails which tell of his middle-class status, but something stops me, and tonight I'm not feeling myself.

"I was drawn to you," I tell him, watching as those eyes flick up with surprise. "As soon as I stepped onto the carnival grounds, my feet would let me go nowhere else. It was a straight line for you."

He's shocked into silence, staring at me with confusion. I never speak like this to Ford. There's never any affection between us, even though we've known each other from a very young age.

"Do you remember when we first met?" I ask him as I reach forward and flick one of the bells on his hat.

His shoulders are stiff, his body vibrating with tension, and I just want to rip off my silk jacket and scrub at his face, taking that ridiculous paint off. I want to know what his expression is because all I see in his eyes is suspicion.

"Of course I remember." He looks around us, finally noticing how far off we are behind the tent, how secluded and dark it is. The carnival still sounds from the other side of the tent, the noise carrying over as if we're still in the center of it.

"Tell me," I demand as I step closer to him. "Tell me about when we first met." I know Ford is envious of my life. I know our friendship has been teetering on a shaky foundation lately, mostly because this year our differences have become prominent. He has to work to support his family, one, two, and now three jobs, whereas I stay at home with my crates of wine and my cartons of cigarettes and waste my days away. The extremes between our lifestyles are beginning to bubble to the surface, and as much as I see envy there, I'm also starting to sense disrespect.

"You ran from your parents," he begins, his voice sounding bored. "Probably because they didn't buy you something you wanted, or maybe they asked you to do something for them. Everyone knows Monty only does for himself."

There it is, the dripping disdain in his words, the flair of jealousy in his chocolate brown eyes. "Go on." I wave him on.

"You ended up at the canal, and in my father's gondola, demanding he give you a ride." A snort flies from his mouth as his arms cross over his chest, diminishing the distance between our bodies. My chest presses against his forearms and I don't dare move an inch back.

"He gave me that ride," I murmur. "All around the canals of Venice. He let me cry the entire ride without asking me a question, and when we pulled up to the dock—"

"I was there," he cuts me off. "I was there with his lunch, and when I saw you for the first time, your despair seemed heavy enough to sink my father's boat."

"We've been inseparable since we were seven years old," I remind him. "Nothing ever came between us, and I don't want that to change."

"Why would that change? Because I'm wearing a jester's hat?" He shakes his head a little, causing the bells to ring, the sound encircling us both like a beautiful wind chime.

His arms drop, opening up the space between us, but I quickly eat it up in one short stride, bringing us nose to nose. Being this close to his face effectively shuts out the painted mask, and I'm drowning in his eyes. The same brown eyes that are slowly burning with curiosity.

"I always want us to be this close," I whisper to him, knowing he can hear me over the sounds of the carnival. "Just like this, Ford. So close that nothing can ever come between us."

"I can smell the amontillado on your breath, and it makes me want to vomit. How drunk are you?"

"Not drunk at all," I snicker as I lean in a little farther, exhaling my breath along the painted slope of his cheek. Then my mouth comes close to the shell of his ear as I whisper, "Just half a bottle."

It's intimate, the way we're standing together, and I expect him to step back to put a little space between us, but he surprises me with the sharp intake of his breath, igniting a warmth deep inside of me.

"I should get back," he whispers, his hand landing on my bicep to ease me back a step.

"I'll go find the girls and see if they found you yet." I grin at him, and when our eyes meet, like the ocean cascading along the dark wet sand, I find the warmth that's been ignited inside of me reflecting in his irises.

Ford gives me a sharp nod and quickly averts his gaze, then strides back toward his podium. His steps are slow, and he looks over his shoulder at me twice before he disappears back around the front of the tent. I can't explain what it is I'm doing or how I'm feeling, but I think I've just cured my boredom.

I give it a minute, and then I follow the same trail Ford did back out to the carnival. I find him up on his podium, playing the small banjo and doing an exaggerated jig to many people's merriment.

I leave him to amuse his audience as I begin to roam the carnival. Games are set up in booths, clowns are handing out balloon animals, and what appeals to me most are the tents labeled for adults only.

I head to the first one and I'm ushered inside by the clown guarding the door. As soon as the flap closes behind me, darkness descends, and smoke fills the tight confines. The low drum beat of the music overrides the noise just outside of the fabric walls, penetrating my ribs and jumpstarting my heart. Everyone is standing around, all of them looking forward, their bodies vibrating with antic-ipation. A red light turns on, cascading over us in a slow roll of seduction.

A female form begins to walk forward on a plat-form, her face covered with a mask, but her body bare for our perusal. She stops in the center of the stage and holds up her arms, showing us they're tied with twine, the lead hanging at the end touching near her toes. Around her neck is a thick leather collar with grizzly spikes adorning the surface.

Her body shimmers in an iridescent dust, and her dusty rose nipples are taut, eliciting a few groans from the men crowded inside the tent. The crowd hushes suddenly, as two men join her on stage. Both of them are slowly stalking toward her from either side, each sporting a black mask and nothing else.

They crowd around her, their hands skimming her body, fingers pinching her nipples and then sinking inside her wet pussy as I stand there transfixed on the debauchery in front of me.

I'm not unaffected as my own cock hardens, then presses against the thin material of my pants. But it isn't until one man reaches out and grabs the other's cock in his large hand, giving it a few pumps, that my cock begins to seep fluid from its tip. I long to reach down inside the waistband to grab my aching genitals and provide it the relief it's begging for.

The man on stage continues to pump his partner's cock in his hand while they both pleasure the woman between them. When cum shoots from the tip, landing on the woman's stomach and the other man's arm, the scene in front of me changes. The female disappears, and it's my cock in Ford's hand.

FORD

His scent didn't make me want to vomit, I lied.

I've tried to perform to earn the wages I've been offered, but since Monty pulled me behind that tent, my mind has been a kaleidoscope of what ifs and what nows. Something happened. A shift has been created. There's a new tether that slipped between my ribs to grip my heart, and the other end is currently attached to my best friend.

Maybe he's more inebriated than he led on, but I saw the clarity in his eyes during our whole inter-action, and now my stomach is knotted, twisting with what ifs and what nows.

Was it because my face was painted? Making it easier for him to change our dynamic? Maybe combined with the alcohol and atmosphere, he's feeling something beyond this dimension. Has he grasped my envy of his life and twisted it much like my stomach, turning it into something he can control? Maybe.

But I will admit, he has stepped into the role of puppeteer, and I am nothing more than his marionette.

"Ford!" I hear Christina call out, her voice husky. The usual raspiness of her tone usually heightens all my sensations, but tonight I find myself annoyed that she's here. I just want to find Monty and figure out what the fuck is going on.

"We found you!" Diana screams, her voice like shattering glass.

I finish wiping the makeup off my face and look up at them both, giving them a curious stare. "It's the end of the night," I tsk. "I fear you've lost this game."

"Diana was sure you were at the kissing booth," Christine admits as she comes to stand between my spread legs. I look up at her from my perch on the end of the podium and slowly raise my brow.

"And is that where you've been all night?"

Her cheeks grow rosy as Diana slaps a hand over her mouth, shock tearing through the dark brown of her eyes.

"You don't own me, Ford." Christina lifts her chin with defiance. "We haven't claimed any sort of ownership. Have we?"

"I guess not." I shrug, feigning nonchalance as my stomach flips with turbulence.

"Poor Monty," Christina snickers, her voice saturated with arrogance. "I bet he is still looking for you."

"Monty found me soon after you guys showed up," I admit to her, enjoying the way her face falls with surprise.

My eyes lock on to a movement just over Christina's shoulder. Monty is sauntering toward us, his hands deep in his pockets, pulling his pants taut across his pelvis. His eyes are downcast, watching the ground in front of him as his shirt moves in the breeze. He's dressed in all black, the cuffs of his shirt rolled up just under his elbows, and his forearms flexing with each step. His curls lift in a sway of motion as the wind slips by him, giving him a godly appearance.

I've always been aware of Monty. Could always sense him when he was nearby, but this tonight is something altogether different. I don't know what he has kindled inside of me, but this fire he started is only being stoked as he draws closer.

"Ladies," he rasps. "You found him."

"Apparently, you found him first." Christina rolls her eyes, but I don't miss the appreciative look she gives him beforehand.

"That's because Ford and I have a connection beyond the physical," he tells them, his finger pressing to the center of his chest. Only reminding me of that tether I feel.

"How romantic," Diana snickers.

"Perhaps in a way." Monty smiles, the gesture anything but friendly. His eyes narrow with a sinister look. "Are you jealous?"

Diana scoffs, but she can't hide the deep blush that blooms across her cheeks.

"Anyway, let's head back to my place." Monty claps his hands. "I have a case of amontillado that I need to finish. You three can help me."

"I want no more of that." I shake my head. "Besides, your parents will kill you."

"They'd have to care to kill me." He throws me a wink and just that simple gesture is filled to the brim with suggestion. These feelings I'm having, the constant thoughts, are shining a light on my best friend, distorting our relationship.

"Yeah, I'll come back to your place," I say with a quick shrug of my shoulders. "I just need to get changed first." I point to the fabric of the jester's costume.

"Keep it on." His words end in a dark chuckle, the sound rolling over me and turning up the heat on the feelings he ignited earlier.

"Not if I'm going to be vomiting later."

I leave them and their laughter behind me as I head toward one of the smaller tents lining the outer perimeter of the carnival. The grounds are a bit more eerie when most of the carnival goers have left for the night. Flickering lights and too-cheerful music sound more intense without the cover of laughter and chatter.

Once I'm dressed back in my street clothes, I exit the tent with the jester costume tucked under my arm, the bells on the hat jingling as I walk toward Monty and the girls. There's no denying the tension between them. The two girls stand off farther to the left, their heads tucked together as they whisper to each other, and Monty is a good ten feet away, his back to them in the utmost dismissal as he stares up at the cloudless night sky.

As if he senses my presence, his face slowly turns toward me, his curls kissing the bottom of his ears as they swing with the motion. Both crystal blue eyes hit me with an intensity half buried beneath hooded eyelids, and my heart kicks up, pounding into my rib cage. There's no mistaking our friendship has been irrevocably changed. By the look of the slow climbing smirk on his face, Monty knows exactly what he's done.

"Let's go." He turns and heads toward the exit, confident the three of us will follow. And so he should be, because the three of us look at each other, knowing tonight, we want to be in the presence of Monty Marcato.

"I won't be able to drink," Christina states as her small hand slips into mine. "I cannot stay the night, nor can I go home drunk."

"I understand." I squeeze her hand and wait for the usual reaction. My stomach will flip, or my heart will squeeze, and heat will travel along my skin. But tonight, there's nothing. Her soft palm against my calloused one invokes absolutely nothing.

"Nor can I," Diana pipes up. "I have to be at the salon in the morning."

Diana's family owns a very popular spa here in Venice, and for five out of the seven days a week, she works there with her mother and two sisters, dyeing, primping, and cutting women's hair.

"Maybe the ladies should just go home," Monty says over his shoulder, proving he can hear everything we're saying.

I watch as Diana's shoulders deflate with disappointment. She has feelings for Monty, and they've only grown more intense over the last year. The looks she gives him have gone from simple interest to clear longing, and there's no mistaking the deep blush that coats her from forehead to chest whenever he looks at her or talks to her.

"Maybe we can do something tomorrow?" I offer. "I don't have to be at the carnival until two o'clock."

Diana's shoulders tip in an uninterested gesture, her eyes still trained to the back of Monty's curly head.

"You can stay at my house tonight," Christina offers. "We can watch movies."

Diana slowly nods, those shoulders of hers remaining tipped forward with the weight of rejection, and I curse myself for losing that bet last night. Now Monty doesn't have to do anything when it comes to hanging out with these girls.

"Drop them off!" Monty calls out as we approach Christina's driveway. "You and I have a date with a bottle of amontillado."

My stomach flips with his words, and it has nothing to do with the hangover that's still lingering.

He's being a good boy and doing exactly what I say. I watch as he walks the girls up the driveway, the fucking jangling of his hat ringing into the silent night. I slip my hands into my pockets, the slight trembling giving away the anxiety I'm feeling. Or is it anticipation? Maybe a little of both. I flip back and forth, wanting to see how far I can take this new dynamic between Ford and me, and being worried that I'm like a freight train moving at top speed. Nothing but inevitable destruction awaits at the end of the track.

Did he kiss her?

I squint my eyes as I watch Christina and Ford embrace, leaving Diana off to the side. Her doe-like eyes never waver from my form. It's annoying. I can smell her desperation from here. There has to be a way to let these women know that men like to be enticed. Don't chase them, don't beg them. Be cruel, ignore them, make them feel like they're at the end of a long line of suitors. Entice them with your appeal, even if it's only a sham.

Like the gentleman he is, Ford stands on that front porch as both girls disappear inside the house, the doorway sealing with the heavy oak door. Then he stands a few seconds longer, staring at the ornate paneling, probably feeling the laser focus of my eyes on his back. What is he thinking? Is he trying to figure out a way to get out of this?

As he turns, a breeze gusts by, lifting his brown hair and tousling it over his forehead. He runs his fingers through the unruly waves as his brows crinkle in the center, but his eyes stay downcast, refusing to meet my own. Frustration bubbles up inside of me because I know it would be easier not to be this curious. To let whatever it is brewing die and tell him to take his ass home. Maybe if I squash it now, we'll both wake up in the morning, having seemingly forgotten all the events leading up to this moment.

My mouth opens, my throat tensing, intending to speak, when his eyes finally lift to meet mine. I must be imagining things because that can't be a look of mischief on his face. He strides forward, his steps eating up the space between us in no time, and sure enough, when he is nearly standing chest to chest with me, his eyes twinkle. The dark brown depths are like pools of chocolate.

"Let's make a bet." The words are taunting, marking my sentiment from yesterday, but spoken with a velvet rasp.

"What's the bet?" I croak, my throat suddenly dry, and my eyes unblinking, for fear this is all a dream. Soon I'm going to wake up in a world I once again hate.

"The first one to pass out becomes a slave for the day to the other."

Even though the word slave is lacking the prefix *sex*, my cock thickens in my pants with the suggestion. Knowing he doesn't have an excellent track record with drinking only tells me he's begging to lose and become my sex slave.

"You're on." I smirk. "I hope you have a good pair of knee pads," I throw over my shoulder as I lead the way back to my house.

"Why? Are you going to make me scrub your floors?" he asks with an exaggerated chuckle.

"No, not my floors." *My cock.*

The silence around us crackles with a volatile energy. Neither of us speaks a single word as we walk under the canopy of stars, our shoes echoing off the cobblestone beneath our feet. I can't help but feel like we're on the edge of an explosion, and neither of us is going to survive the internal combustion.

The heat alone emanating from our pores is enough to ignite an inferno.

We turn on to my driveway, the fucking bells on his hat still jangling with each step, and I look up at my house. I look at the darkened windows and the atmosphere of dread begins to descend upon me. Empty. The house is empty, I'm empty. Everything is empty.

And I almost fall into that pit again of self-loathing, of boredom and anger until those fucking bells ring. My eyes skip to the side to see Ford's profile. My sight lingers on the straight line of his nose and how his top lip is slightly plumper than the bottom, giving him a tragic pout.

"I used to be afraid of your house when we were kids." I watch as his lips move with each syllable, my eyes burning from the lack of blinking. "It always felt too big for your family, and then there's the fucking catacombs in your basement." Finally, his head turns, and his eyes spear me in place on the driveway.

"I'm the only monster in that house," I tell him. "It's always been me."

"I'm not disagreeing with you there," he snorts and then begins to walk ahead, heading toward my front door. With one last look at the expansive façade of my empty house, I let out a sigh and follow behind him.

I wasn't lying when I told him I'm the only monster who resides inside these empty walls. "You'll soon find out just how true that statement is."

He goes straight for the kitchen, grumbling that I've already brought up more of the amontillado.

C.A. RENE

"You should eat first this time," I advise when he pulls the cork out of the half-finished bottle fitting on the island.

"Are you going to cook for me again?" His head tips, sending his dark hair tumbling to the side. "This is starting to feel like a date, Monty."

Ford knows I don't date. There's no need. I'm a man who enjoys my solitude. Most women know that, and for the ones who don't, I leave it all plain and clear on the table in front of them. Most of the time, it's just one night and one night only.

"If that's what I got to do to get you in bed," I snicker. It's meant as a joke, at least I think it is, but when the only sound to follow my laugh is of him gulping the wine in quick succession, I realize he's reading a lot further into it.

What's the point of correcting him? Just maybe that's what will happen, anyway.

Or we'll both come to our senses and snap out of whatever sorcery has befallen us tonight.

I make a quick bruschetta, then I dice some tomato and onion to sprinkle on top. It's one of Ford's favorites and he's always indulged our cook's homemade bread since the first day he walked into my home.

He scarfs down a few slices while I top off his glass and fill the second one for myself. His fingers wrap around the stem with determination, and for the first time, I feel like maybe I'll lose this bet. And if I do, how would he utilize me as his slave?

"She's in love with you." His finger sways unsteadily as he tries to point it in my face. "I cannot commit myself to a woman who's in love with my best friend."

"Christina is not in love with me," I assure him as I top off his glass, which polishes off this second bottle of wine.

"She is." He nods, the motion making his jowls bounce as his mouth turns downward. "I see the way she watches you. It's not as bad as Diana, but it goes beyond intrigue."

"Can I ask you something?" I lean forward as the room spins on its axis. "Does it bother you if she's in love with me?"

He sways on his perch at the end of the couch, his hand sloppily grabbing the wineglass and bringing the rim to his mouth. His throat pulses with each gulp he takes, and I stare, stunned, as he places the empty glass back on the table in front of him.

"Yes, it bothers me, but not for the reasons you think. I am not in love with Christina," he admits. "I know one day I am expected to marry, and my parents can only hope that match is beneficial for our family, but I'd still like her to look at me with at least as much interest as Christina looks at you."

"It's probably because of my handsome face." I wave my hand around the air as I try my best to infuse this depressing topic with some humor.

"It is a handsome face." He nods as his eyes nearly seal shut.

My stomach flips, but my patience has come to an abrupt end, and I find myself leaning over to wrap my hand around his throat, squeezing until his eyes pop open.

"Say it again," I demand as I drag him in closer to me, his hands scrambling to find purchase on the couch cushions.

"Monty!" he exclaims just as his nose bounces into mine. "What are you doing?"

With the bravery stemming from the dark liquid we've consumed; I forget all words of explanation and seal my mouth over his.

FORD

Kissing a man is so different from kissing a woman. The scrape of his scruff scores against my top lip, contrasting with the soft press of his lips. There's no desperation, no frantic movements, just the both of us slowly easing into foreign territory and experiencing something for the very first time. Unlike being a child and absorbing it through rose-colored glasses, we're adults and analyzing every single aspect.

Kissing a man is very similar to kissing a woman. The way our tongues glide along the rough surfaces, ensnaring with one another, the soft press of plush lips, and the experience of tasting another person for the very first time. All of that is similar to a woman, except the rough scrape of two-day-old growth is an added sensation. Large hands grip the nape of your neck. The touch is nothing like the sweet skim of a woman's skin, and finally there's this scent. Like musk after a heavy rainstorm, dark and earthy. There's no hint of sweetness in the air surrounding us, and therefore, there's no reason to close my eyes and imagine I'm anywhere else but sitting on this couch and kissing my best friend.

He must be feeling similar as both of our eyes are wide open, my cock is painfully hard, pulsing in my pants and begging for a release. I know it's going to be different, and with little thought, I reach forward to grasp his cock through his thin pants. More for curiosity. I want to see if he is just as affected as I am.

Monty pulls back from my mouth, our breaths mingling in the tiny space between us. Heavy pants ramp up the heat we're feeling as my hand continues to grip around his hard length. He wants this too.

Only I'm not sure what this is, where it's going to go, and most importantly, how it's going to end.

"A bottle and a half have us making out like adolescents and feeling each other up," he laughs nervously, drawing back away from me, and easing his groin away from my hand. "We still have another bottle."

My head is swimming from how fast I drank the first, and I'm not sure if another bottle is necessary. A part of me is thinking maybe it's necessary for Monty. Perhaps this has all been a grand scheme for him, thinking I wouldn't have ever let it get this far, so I nod my head.

He watches me from under hooded lids, his lips working as he ponders, or maybe he's scrutinizing me. I'm not sure, but I sit still and let exactly what I'm feeling emanate from the features of my face. I'm hot, I'm fucking bothered, and I want to jam my cock so far down his throat that I'm willing to wait for him to drink a bottle of wine to accept it.

"What's happening?" he asks as his fingers tentatively touch his lips, the pads dragging over the soft skin, reddened from my mouth.

"You tell me." I shake my head. "You're the one who started this. Does it have to be me to finish it?"

Monty may be lazy, he may be so fucking full of himself, but he's competitive as fuck. So when his eyebrows crease together with a look of determination, I know I may live to regret my words.

"How will we determine who is a slave?" He tips his head to the side, reminding me of the bet that has somehow slipped my mind.

"I'll be your slave," I tell him. "Now I understand why you wanted me to have knee pads." My own fingers come up to brush along my mouth, mirroring his movements, only my gesture is filled with suggestion.

His blue eyes darken as his teeth sink into his bottom lip, with what I can only assume are images of me on my knees flooding his mind. So as my vision spins around me, I slip off the couch and onto my knees, working my way between his legs.

Monty's chest heaves with labored breaths, and his fingers twitch as they rest on his thighs, but right there in his eyes, I can see his excitement swirling with trepidation. I don't give him much time to think because even though he did start this, he's lit something inside me I didn't know existed. Just maybe this whole time, the disdain I was feeling for my best friend was a mere frustration at not acting on my desires.

His pants are drawstring, smooth linen, thin against my touch. His heat easily radiates through the thin material. I pull on the string, watching as the tie comes undone with ease, and then with my eyes firmly on his, I wrap my fingers around the waistband of his pants, gripping his boxers with them and I give them a yank.

Monty doesn't immediately move for me, and even though we're nestled inside a cloud of lust and need, there's also a storm brewing on the horizon, carrying with it a slight tinge of fear. Whereas I'm ready to be swept up by the monsoon of desire, he's afraid of drowning.

I watch him closely, and I see the second he relents. The way his lips curve upward, and his hips lift just enough for me to slip his pants down. They pool around his ankles, my eyes avoiding what I know is waiting for me between his legs. Obviously I've never done this before, but it's been done to me plenty of times. I'm sure I can work out the logistics of it. I'm just unsure. What if he doesn't like it?

"Suck my cock, Ford."

His words have my eyes flying up to meet his, making me suddenly remember this is my best friend, and he knows me better than anyone else. So of course he could sense everything I'm feeling.

His hand wraps around his long thick length, and I swallow down the sudden jolt of surprise. I think Monty's cock is bigger than mine. Which is absurd because I am enormous. His dark chuckle hits my ears as I begin to lean forward. Again, he's sensing exactly what I'm thinking, but I refuse to give in and squabble with him about length and girth. I'm dying to know what it'll be like to have his satin smooth skin slipping along my tongue, how his cock will taste, and mostly, if I'll enjoy it.

So, without further hesitation, I take my best friend's advice, and I suck his cock deep down my throat. I let the wide mushroom tip bounce against the sensitive flesh, causing me to retch around his length, but it's the sound of his guttural groan that spurs me onward. I hollow out my cheeks as I've watched Christina do many times, and cushion his girth with warm flesh, then I bob up and down, running my tongue over that spot I know drives men insane. It fucking drives me insane. His hands slip into the thick strands of my hair, his fingers pressing into my scalp as he forces my head down more, thrusting upward to sink himself even deeper.

Finally I just loosen my jaw and let him do exactly what he pleases. By the end of this, my esophagus will probably be bruised, but seeing how euphoric his face is makes it all worth it.

Saliva drips from my mouth, sliding down his shaft to nestle against his balls and slapping against my chin. With my eyes closed, the sounds almost remind me of fucking a woman and it makes me painfully hard.

"You feel so fucking good, baby," he groans as he continues to assault my mouth. "So warm and so fucking wet."

His thrusts become sloppy but more forceful, and with every withdrawal, I suck in a breath just to keep from passing out. What a torturously plea-surable way to go, though.

"I'm about to fill this mouth up with cum," he growls as his fingers curl tighter into my hair. "I want to hear you swallow every fucking drop."

I'm nodding as he fucks my throat raw, knowing when I finally do swallow it's going to be the sweetest pain I've ever experienced. And just like a virgin girl, I'll feel him there for the next few days.

"Look at me while I'm fucking you," he snaps, and my eyes move like lightning to focus on his as the tears distort my vision. "So fucking hot, Ford."

His jaw tenses while he thrusts into my mouth one last time. The tip of his cock is firmly rooted into my throat as his salty cum squirts out thick spurts, and just like I thought, with every constriction of my throat, pain radiates all the way up to my jaws. Still, I swallow every drop and then lick him clean afterward.

CHAPTER
FIVE

MONTY

I t's been two weeks since I fucked Ford's mouth, and for the past two weeks, we've been inseparable. We wake up, we suck each other's dicks, he goes to work, I beat off to the thought of fucking his mouth when he's off work. Then he comes to my house. We drink wine, and we're fucking each other's mouths until we pass out. It's the farthest we've gone in our experimentation, and so far we're comfortable. We're enjoying each other and there's no pressure to go farther.

Only the thought of sinking my cock into his tight asshole has become a point of obsession for me.

If I thought for one second Ford was ready to take that next step with me, I'd hold him down in bed and force my way inside him. As intriguing as that is, I'm already walking a fine line of patience, not wanting to completely decimate our friendship, but on the other hand, constantly finding ways to have him naked and violating him anyway I can.

Our bond has solidified beyond the scope of friendship, and as each day passes, I find myself more entangled in the web Ford is spinning. Even though he has no idea exactly what he's doing, he's having fun just as he's always had with every one of his conquests, but I vow to change that.

Before him, I was nothing but an empty shell, and then he showed me what it was to have a friend. Just when my life was becoming mundane, repetitive, and utterly boring, he painted me a picture in vivid colors.

The carnival will be wrapping up in two weeks. They will pack away the tents, take down the rides, pull apart the kiosks, and once again, the nights will be filled with silence as they ride away, taking the laughter and cheer with them.

I can only hope it doesn't take away what's happening between Ford and me.

We would never be accepted. Both of our families are way too traditional to understand this new dynamic we've been exploring, but we don't need them. If we had to, we could get our own place. I would support him, and he could be a clown, a jester, a mechanic. Fuck, he could sell gondola rides like his father, despite that, I'd be content for once in my life.

I step through the gates of the carnival and let myself be immersed in a world of games and fried foods. To let the music sing to my soul and absorb the laughter of children as they run from ride to ride.

The sun hasn't yet set, but there on the podium is Ford, with his face makeup and jester outfit. He's dancing and playing with his small banjo. I pause to watch him, taking in the scene in front of me. The crowd encircles him, clapping along with his antics and laughing when he pretends to nearly fall off the edge. He's enrapturing all of them, luring them into another web he's spinning, and the smile slowly falls from my face as jealousy scorches through me, igniting my limbs in heat.

He is mine.

My erratic emotions are sending me for a tailspin, so instead of approaching him and his admiring crowd, I head back toward the adult tent I was in the first night I discovered Ford. I breathe out the possessive feelings. I don't want to ruin the fragile relationship we're building.

I approach the man standing by the tent flap and he gives me a quick once-over, nodding his head and permitting my entry.

It's dark, like the first time, only now there aren't so many people in here. Mostly it's men, which makes sense. This is no tent for a lady. The provocative scenes portrayed on stage are only meant for the most deviant.

I approach closer to the stage, keeping myself along the edge of the tent, shrouding myself in the darkness and avoiding the dim ambient light. I only want to watch and forget the dangerous feelings building inside me.

A spotlight comes on at the edge of the platform, beaming its light dead center, and two men walk on stage. Both of them are wearing a collar with a chain hanging from the center with what look to be black satin bags over their heads and nothing else. My eyes trail over their bodies with curiosity, trying to see if the sight of their flaccid cocks does anything for me. They don't. Then I skim over the tightly packed muscles of their stomachs, back along bulging biceps, but still nothing. It seems the only man I'm crumbling to my knees for is Ford. I bet he would love to hear that, but I can never tell him.

A whistle sounds, making the men stop abruptly while they face each other, standing about a foot apart. I'm expecting the woman to come out like the first show, but I'm shocked further when another man steps out, his face painted eerily similar to Ford's, and he too is wearing a jester's outfit. My heart begins to beat fast and hard, and red hues begin to seep into the edges of my vision, igniting a rage so hot I fear I'm about to burn this whole carnival to the fucking ground.

Surely that is not Ford. I just left him on his podium, entertaining his people. Logically, I know that's where he is, and that Ford would never partake in such activities.

I know it, but as I watch him open the front flap of his pants to pull out his cock, I try my best to squint and see if it's the cock that I know so well.

A growl of frustration slips from my throat when the light on stage dims and both men on either side of the jester fall to their knees. The holes in the hood are used to pleasure the jester. His cock disappears into the hood of the man on the right, while the other slips behind him to please the one place I have yet to claim on Ford.

As the debauchery continues on stage, my eyes stay focused on his painted face, only pulling out more irritation because I can't seem to see the features. Damn Ford for having no distinguishing feature. His eyes are brown, just like the man on stage, straight perfect nose, no bumps on the bridge, and lips concealed in black paint.

I cannot tell if this is Ford or not, but to keep myself rooted in my spot in the shadows, I convince myself he's still outside. If I listen hard enough, I can hear the laughter and the jingle of his hat. And that's when it hits me. The man on stage doesn't have a hat, because there can only be one true jester at the carnival. The solace is immediate, dosing the jealous flames and bathing me in icy cool relief.

The three men on stage pleasure each other in the most forbidden ways, and I look around the tent, finding men with their own cocks in their hands, absorbing the pleasure in which they could never express in public beyond this tent. Not without being judged and sometimes persecuted for it.

I crave to take my own cock out. It's hard and pulsing, pressing painfully to the zipper of my chinos, but I don't because the essence that comes from the tip is meant for one person only, and I decide tonight I'm going to fill his ass with it.

As I back away from the stage, the men all stand in a row with the jester in the center. The hooded man to the right grabs the jester's face, dragging him forward, his thumb leaving behind smudged black paint. I'm just about to open the flap when a hand grabs my bicep. I turn to find the guard that was outside the tent as he puts something into my hand before letting me leave.

I step out into the night and suck in a lungful of fresh air, breathing in the scents of the carnival around me. Then I open the palm of my hand

and look down. There in the center of it lies a condom and a small tube of lube.

He thought I was gay.

But am I?

I think about what I saw in there, and my only reactions were jealousy, rage, and then relief. The only time I felt desire was when I thought of Ford.

Ford.

I head to the podium, my mouth tipping upward when I hear the familiar jingles, and then my cock jerks in my pants, reminding me of the filthy things I plan to do to my best friend.

As I get closer to the podium, I see two familiar faces staring up at my friend, and another hot poker slams between my ribs, filling the space with jealousy again. Christina and Diana are laughing and clapping along with Ford's antics, and I grit my teeth until I hear a distinct grinding sound. For the past two weeks, I've effectively kept them apart. She's been calling him nonstop, but most of those times, I had his mouth filled with my cock. It seems she's gone to desperate measures to get his attention by showing up here.

I can't approach them like this, with rage boiling through my blood and jealousy like a potent poison, slipping its way through my heart and threatening to kill me with its venom. I will do nothing but destroy our already fragile foundation.

I'd might as well wrap Ford in a bow and hand him off to Christina.

I gravitate toward the massive Ferris wheel, its flashing lights beckoning me like the moth to the flame. One ride should calm me, and I can go back and collect my best friend and get rid of those bitches like I did two weeks ago.

Thankfully, the line is quite short when I get there, and after five minutes, I'm swooped into an empty cart and the door locked tight. When it begins to move, the wheel ascending toward the sky; I lean back in the plastic seat and focus on the stars above my head. The carriage stops with a groan, my cart swinging precariously back and forth. I lean up and look over the edge, and there on the center podium are Christina and Ford, sitting cross legged facing each other with him strumming that banjo.

Is he serenading her?

She reaches out, pushing his hair out of his face, and letting it curl around the tips of her fingers. I know in this instant, there's no calming the storm. As soon as this cart opens, I'm engulfing them both.

As soon as my feet hit soil, I rush toward that podium, the scenes in front of me pulsing with the heavy beat of my heart. All of it distorted by a rhythm of rage.

"Monty?"

I turn abruptly to see Ford standing behind the tent, that fucking hat in his hand, as he gingerly wipes the makeup off his forehead.

I rush forward, grabbing his jaws in my hand and smearing the black paint down his cheek farther. "What the fuck are you trying to do?"

His eyes widen with surprise. "What do you mean?"

FORD

He doesn't say anything more, instead cutting off my words and crashing his mouth to mine. It's been a game of back and forth these last few weeks. He dominates. I fight back. I dominate. He fights back, but there has always been a playful undertone to it. Right now, there's nothing playful about the way he's devouring me.

His hand is sealed around my throat, squeezing as he growls into my mouth. It feels like complete and utter possession.

Regardless, it doesn't halt my reaction as I grow hard in my thin pants, and we both stumble from the force of his attack, making my ass meet the wooden crate behind me. His hand rips into the front flap of my outfit, surprising me that he even knows it's there, and he grabs my steel length in his hand, the squeeze brutal and hauling me in closer.

I don't know what's setting him off, but I don't dislike it, and the fact that we could be so easily caught only heightens the moment.

Monty's teeth nip into my lip, the sudden pain sharp as the taste of iron floods my tongue. I heave and try to draw away, but his hand is still sealed around my throat and keeps me rooted to the spot as he continues to ravage my mouth.

The brutality of this kiss is searing through my body, making me crave more. The feeling is so strong that I know if his mouth wasn't sealed over mine, I'd be begging him for just that.

His mouth rips away, and his eyes burn red with anger. The blue completely darkens. "Turn around," he demands.

My first instinct is to fight him, to tell him no and shove him off me. Not only are we in a public place but turning around means I'm submitting. It means I'm going to let him fuck me for the first time behind a tent at a carnival. A place where the ambience is flickering neon lights and creepy lilting music.

Unfortunately, before I even have time to think up an argument, I've already turned around. My hands are pressed into the wooden crates and Monty's chuckle is humorless as his hands skim down over my ass cheeks. His fingers run along my crack, roughly causing me to tense.

"Relax, this is going to hurt," he snarks.

"Of course it's going to hurt," I snap and look at him over my shoulder. "We have nothing here."

"And yet here you are, bent over like a fucking slut." Monty's palm cracks against my ass cheek, and I hiss through the pain. "What were you doing back here?" he asks as he pulls away the flap, exposing my asshole to the cool air. "Were you taking off your makeup? And then what? Were you going to go and grab Christina to finish what you were starting?"

"What were we starting?" I question, confusion saturating my words.

"Don't try to talk your way out of this one." I hear his pants being opened and then the distinct rip of a condom wrapper. "I saw you two."

"Why do you have a condom on you?" Now it's my turn to sound crazy with jealousy. He and I haven't been fucking, so why the fuck is he here with a condom in his pocket?

"It was given to me," he growls.

I'm still processing that information when I feel him squirt something cool against my asshole, and then shock tears through me. I know exactly where he got this, but before I can open my mouth, he's pushing inside me. The burn is immediate as it radiates up and throughout my body, but I grit my teeth. Even though it hurts, the feeling of having him inside me is something I've never experienced. I'm not completely sure if I like it, but I like that it's him.

Besides, it'll be my turn later.

"Put that hat on your head."

I couldn't have heard him right, I think to myself as my eyes skip to the hat sitting on top of the wooden crates, the bells slightly jingling every time he thrusts into me.

"Now," he snaps as he slams into me and stills, his cock pulsing and my asshole clenching around him.

I reach my hand out to grab the hat, partly out of anger and partly because I'm intrigued. I pull it over my head, then look over my shoulder to find him watching the hat intently as the bells chime with the movement. Then a slow, crawling smile creeps over his mouth, sending chills down my spine. His hand reaches forward, grabbing onto the satin cap and gripping it tighter to my head.

The sound of girls laughing has my heart pounding into my rib cage because Christina and Diana are just on the other side of this tent. I don't know if Monty hears them or not, but he continues plowing into me as I reach between my legs to grab my own cock. I begin jerking it off to the sound of the laughter, and the fact that I'm being fucked for the first time outside in the middle of a carnival.

The burn begins to subside and pleasure courses through me. My cock jerks in my hand as Monty's thrusts become sloppy, a telltale sign that he's nearing his end. With two last thrusts, the hat jingles a melody, playing a tune of debauchery and depravity, and the sound sets off my own release, causing Monty and I to groan at the exact same time.

Cum squirts from my dick onto the wooden crates as Monty's dick jerks with the final bits of his release. Everything around us becomes a little clearer, and it finally hits me just exactly what we've done and where we've done it.

"Get out of me." I grab the hat off my head, the bells protesting as I slam it down on top of the crates. "What the fuck is your problem?"

"I'm getting tired of seeing you with Christina."

"I am dating Christina," I reiterate as I spin around. "Of course she's here with me."

"Whatever." He rolls his eyes and tucks himself back in his pants, dropping the used condom on the crate beside my hat. "Are you coming to my house?"

I'm pissed off and I just want to tell him to go fuck himself, that no, I won't be coming to his house tonight. Even though we've been spending every night together for the last two weeks.

But I'm weak and I want nothing more than to spend the night with him again.

"Yeah," I tell him as I grab up the wipes and continue to clean my face. "I just need to get changed and drop Christina home."

"Don't take too long, then." He grabs up the jester's hat and tucks it under his arm. "This will be waiting for you there."

The front door, opening and shutting, wakes me from my distorted dreams of jingling hats and screams of pain. I know before I even open my eyes, it's Ford leaving for whatever job he has at such an ungodly hour. With my arms over my head, I stretch my body, feeling the delicious soreness throughout my legs.

He fucked me good last night.

"Was that your front door?"

The sound of his sleepy voice beside me on the bed has my eyes snapping open as I throw the blankets off my body. Either someone has just walked unannounced into my home, or my parents are back. Neither is a welcomed presence.

"Get out of my bed. I think my parents are home." I snap my fingers as I grab a robe.

The sounds of them in the kitchen, the cabinets banging shut, and heels hitting tile, tell me my mother may be on the warpath. I left the amontillado bottles in there, their favorite wine.

I quickly slip out of my room and head to the staircase, listening for their voices, but hearing nothing. Just the *click, click, click* of heels on the tiles. I hit the bottom stair when I see her.

Her usually dark brown hair has been lightened with copper streaks, her skin is glowing with a radiance only acquired by many hours in the sun, and her crystal blue eyes are still as cold and calculating as I remember.

"Hello, little brother."

"Danielle." I nod as I take in my sister's stature.

She's always been tall and willowy, but I can see she's put on some weight. She's filling out her outfit in places she complained she hadn't before.

"Too much bread in France?" I snicker.

She rolls her eyes, making her long black lashes skim against her eyebrows, and lets out a sigh. "When will you grow up, brother?"

A door opening upstairs has her eyes darting upward, curiosity clearly shining through. "Another conquest?"

Ford appears at the top of the stairs in his linen trousers and black button-up top. His hair is tousled, and his eyes still filled with sleep.

"You guys still have sleepovers?" Danielle chuckles. "In the same bed?"

"What are you doing at home?" I interrupt her pestering.

"Didn't mother call you?"

"Of course not," I snort.

"I have graduated from my courses, and now I am here to take over the family business."

It's my turn to roll my eyes at her outrageous assumptions and watch as she gives my best friend another once-over. I can see the interest, something that wasn't there the last time she was home.

Then again, my eyes follow hers. He didn't look this good the last time she was home.

The work at the garage has filled him out, and his once soft jaw is angular and dusted with dark hair.

"How are you, Ford?" Her voice takes on an edge of honey. The coarse way she speaks to me is suddenly smoothed into velvet.

"Late," he says as he makes his way down the stairs. "I should've been at work by now."

"A working man," she hums. "One who understands responsibility. I can see none of that has rubbed off on my brother."

Oh, a lot of what Ford does has rubbed off on me, sister.

"Where are you working?"

"At the garage," he states as he puts on his jacket and shoes. "I'll see you later," he says to me.

Then he disappears out of the door, my sister's cunning eyes watching every movement.

"I do need an oil change," she hums.

My body vibrates with anger, something akin to pure volatile rage, and to ignite the fires further, she ruffles my hair as she passes, heading for the stairs.

"You look absolutely vicious, brother," she observes. "Whatever for?"

"Maybe because you're back and already sticking your nose where it doesn't belong."

"My nose has always and will always belong in your business," she purrs as she slowly climbs the stairs. "It'll do you good to remember that."

Danielle has a darkness stirring inside of her, a need to worm her way into people's lives just to see how she can ruin it. With the exception of our parents. She needs them financially, but me? I'm usually her first target.

I follow her up the stairs, finding her standing in my bedroom doorway, her pert nose turned up in a sneer.

"Did you have a female in here with you?"

"Get out of my room."

"Or was it just you and Ford?" Her eyes widen with suggestion as I push past her, slamming my door in her face. Her husky chuckle trails down the hallway as she heads for her room, the sound like nails on a chalkboard.

I head to my bathroom, noticing Ford's hat sitting on my dresser, and feel myself harden beneath my robe. If my sister finds out what we've been up to, she will stop at nothing to ruin it. Danielle would tell our parents, then soak in the chaos from her actions like a flower beneath the Venetian sun.

The thought of my sister being here only sours my mood further, because that means my mother and father aren't too far behind. Danielle is their golden child, and if she's back from France, they will want to be here with her.

I may be the heir to the Marcato business, much to my father's disdain, but she is the apple of their eye. Whatever Danielle wants, Danielle gets. Like studying fashion in France or driving an Alfa Romeo. Nothing is too extravagant for their precious daughter.

A daughter who is of marrying age and has yet to settle down.

Probably because she's too much to handle. Most men she dates stick around until they see the veritable monster lurking underneath, and no amount of wealth makes them stay. I don't blame them.

I may be lazy and bored out of my fucking mind, but she's just plain evil.

Funny thing is my parents know it. They've been trying to marry her off for years to other diplomats' sons, to friends of the family, to just about anyone, but it always ends up the same way. No one wants to live out their days with Danielle Marcato, no matter the size of the dowry.

I get out of the shower and hear her heeled shoes hitting the hardwood outside of my room door. The *click*, *clack*, struck with purpose. The front door opens and closes in quick succession, and an ominous feeling hits me like a hot poker.

She wanted an oil change.

FORD

Sweat rolls from my temple and over my cheek, leaving a trail of salty coolness in its wake. I would rather be at the carnival than slaving here all day, but unfortunately, it's only in town for a month. In the meantime, I need this job to sustain me for the rest of the year.

"No, I don't have an appointment," a familiar voice huffs. "But an excellent friend of mine works here. Ford Rossi."

"Fuck," I curse under my breath as I drop the towel I was using to wipe the grease off my fingers. Danielle Marcato, being here and seeking me out is bad. She never gave a shit about me before, and her sudden interest can only stem from whatever devious plan she has in place to piss off her brother.

"Rossi!"

I head toward the front desk and find Danielle leaning on the counter, her cream silk blouse no doubt being sullied by the soiled surface.

"Ford." Her mouth puckers as she whines. "I need an oil change. My daddy will be so angry if he finds out I've neglected Romeo."

She's named her fucking car.

Francesco snorts from his seat at the desk, and I flick his ear as I make my way over to the Alfa

Romeo. What I wouldn't give to drive one of these, let alone own one.

"Isn't he a beauty?" Danielle husks into my ear. She's tall, around five feet, nine inches, but in those six-inch heels, she's my height.

"Oil changes are tricky on these guys. It'll take me a bit and it'll be pricey."

"Money isn't an issue." She waves her hand over her head, making her brunette waves sway. "I would pay whatever you want, knowing he's in expert hands."

She grabs up my filthy hands in her pristine ones and gives me a look from under her lashes. My cock stirs in my pants as a wash of shame comes over me. It looks like I'm affected by more than one Marcato.

With how possessive Monty has been lately, I wouldn't put it past him to kill us both if he knew exactly what it was I'm feeling.

It's just arousal at the prospect of a beautiful woman who smells of sunshine, and her deep pockets. Fickle, I know. But it's the truth.

Is that how I feel about Monty? Is that why I'm doing what I am doing with him? Maybe I haven't fully thought it through. I know we don't have a future, but I am attracted to his lifestyle. I just want to feel what it's like to live inside of his orbit for a little while.

That's not so terrible. He must know this isn't serious either. Once we've had our fill, we'll return to Monty and Ford, best friends.

"Call me when the car is ready." She slips a piece of paper into my pants pocket, no doubt brushing along the hardness of my cock.

Then she turns on her heel, causing her hair to flick me in the face, leaving me in a cloud of musk.

"**S**he actually did it." His voice sounds like it's vibrating with disbelief, and unfortunately I can't see his face because I'm under Danielle's car, but I can imagine it's dark and brooding, looking like dark clouds swooping in on a hot summer day.

"Are you talking about your sister bringing her car for an oil change?" I call out.

"You and I both know she is up to something." I hear his fingers begin to tap along the body of the car as he tries to alleviate his rage.

"What could she be up to?" I ask him as my heart begins to pound. "Did you tell her something?"

"Of course I didn't," he scoffs. "But it's Danielle. She's like a shark, and as soon as she gets that single scent of blood, she won't stop until she finds the source."

"Well, I'm sure you can prevent that from happening," I tell him while I grit my teeth with irritation. The fact that he is here and angry that I'm working on his sister's car is irrational, especially when there's a chance that she could figure everything out and expose us for what we're doing. "It seems like your energy is misplaced."

"What do you mean by my energy?"

"You're here instead of trying to defuse whatever it is she thinks she's gotten a scent of."

"Don't encourage her." I hear his palm hit the aluminum. "She's going to flirt with you. Do not encourage it, Ford."

It's becoming claustrophobic being inside Monty's orbit. He's smothering me every chance he can get, and not for the first time, I regret what we've started. It was only supposed to be fun, but it feels like it's taking a turn.

"She's your sister," I remind him. "Why would I tolerate that?"

"I just want to make sure we are on the same page," he growls, and the tenor of his voice grates on my last nerve. He's always demanding, setting the rules, telling me who I can and can't speak to, who I can date. The fact that Christina has been chased off in the last few weeks is irritating at most, nothing devastating. She and I weren't meant to last, but that doesn't mean I was finished with her.

I turn my head and watch as his brown leather loafers walk away from the car and back outside into the Venetian sun. I long to follow him, to be able to walk in his path, not having any responsibilities, and enjoy the sun. Not having to work away my days and be exhausted every night.

I'll probably never know what it's like. I will have to work probably multiple jobs to scrape together whatever money I make and pray it covers my bills. I'll live from paycheck to paycheck, praying nothing bounces in the bank and I'll be able to meet my mortgage, and ensure my children are fed. My wife will probably have to work as well.

I'm destined to repeat the same cycle as my parents, and even though their lives weren't terrible, we had love, we had food on the table, but it's been hard.

There was a part of me that hoped I had won over Christina's parents, that they would consider me as a husband for their daughter, but maybe I was too eager. Maybe the gleam they saw in my eye was for the lifestyle and not love for their daughter, and in that case, I can't blame them.

"Rossi!" Angelo, the other mechanic, calls out. "Your other appointment is waiting. How much longer are you going to be?"

Changing the oil in an Alfa Romeo isn't simple, and it's taken up a good chunk of my day.

"I'm almost done, about ten more minutes."

"No more taking walk-ins." He taps the car and walks away.

His arrogant tone pisses me off, but there's not much I can do about it. He's the senior mechanic here, and if I push against his authority, he'll kick me out as fast as I could tell him exactly how I'm feeling.

S he saunters into the garage with a teal silk scarf wrapped around her head and large dark sunglasses covering her eyes. Her lips are painted a blood red, offsetting the dark olive of her skin. She is wearing a matching sundress, the color making her skin pop and glisten, looking so supple as she makes her way closer to me.

Her breasts bounce and sway without the construction of a bra, and her long red fingernails run along the skin of her throat, gripping at the pure gold chain wrapped around her neck.

Danielle Marcato screams wealth. Where Monty is more subdued and almost annoyed by his financial state, Danielle breathes it.

She stops in front of me, her body so close I can smell the coconut oil off her skin mixed with sunshine. No doubt she was tanning, probably naked by her pool, and just the thought of her not wearing any panties under her silk dress has me hardening in my pants. Her fingers grip my arm, the nails embedding themselves in my skin as she smiles up into my face, my eyes reflecting back at me in her sunglasses.

"Thank you so much, Ford," she coos. "You've saved me from a really long lecture tonight at dinner."

"No problem." I keep my voice even, unaffected by her scent and her touch.

"Won't you come for dinner?" she asks. "I bet Mommy and Daddy would love to see you."

"I'll have to speak to Monty."

"Come as my guest," she suggests. "I won't take no for an answer."

I find myself nodding even as images of Monty stabbing me over the dinner table in front of his family flick through my mind.

I knew it.

I knew Danielle would come here and somehow entice my best friend.

That's not what bothers me the most though. It's Ford standing there looking like a complete idiot and nodding his head to whatever it is she's telling him.

I know the effect my sister has on men. I've watched many fall to their knees in the beginning, only to run in terror a short time later. She's seductive, but she's poison wrapped in a beautiful exterior. My parents are beginning to worry about her future because she's nearing the age of spinster.

The longer I watch them inside the garage, the more my blood boils. She's naked under that dress. I would know, she paraded around the pool without a stitch on and then inside the house.

When I screamed at her to put clothes on, she only laughed and waved me off, saying she'd hoped I had seen a pair of breasts before her own.

She probably smells like coconut oil since that's what she lathered herself with beside the pool, and in the matter of three hours, she grew three shades darker.

Ford is weak, and if she has him in her sights for seduction, he won't survive it.

She always did enjoy slumming it when life became boring, and Ford would be an easy target.

I take a drag on my cigarette and lean against the tree across the street from the garage. I've been out of the house since my parents came home about half an hour ago and decided to follow Danielle here. The garage is about a twenty-minute walk from our house, and I watched as men nearly gave themselves whiplash as my sister strutted down the street. That's always been her prerogative, to gain a man's attention just so she can somehow exploit them.

I never cared about it much before. None of it was my problem, but now that her sights are on my best friend, I have some skin in the game. Ford isn't just my best friend now, he's my lover too.

Her fingers wrap around his arm as her body slides against his, only fanning my flames of anger. Not because of what she's doing, but because Ford is looking at her like she's a goddess.

He is weak.

I take a final drag off my cigarette and drop it to the ground, digging my heel into the cherry and exhaling the smoke through my nose. I could always go by Christina's house and let her know that the man she's seeing has his sights set on my sister, but I don't even know if that would work. Since he's been so wrapped up in me, I think Christina's been pushed to the side.

But if he thinks he can become involved with my sister, maybe I will search out Christina for myself.

I shake my head, clearing those vile thoughts. Jealousy does crazy things to people, and even though Ford looks like a blubbering idiot, he has yet to do anything wrong. Yet here I am, planning revenge as if he's wronged me.

I watch as he walks my sister over to her car, opening the door so she can slip inside, and then he closes it, tapping the hood. He raises his hand in farewell as she pulls out of the garage and heads back toward home, just as the sun begins to lower in the sky.

My parents demanded we be home for dinner so we can all sit down as a family, and I want to invite Ford, but our family dinners are nothing like his. We're cold and detached, and most of my parents' attention will be on Danielle. I'd rather he not witness that.

I make my way up the driveway, seeing my sister's car and my parents' car sitting side by side, the sight of them making my stomach flip with anxiety. I know at times when they are not here, I feel lonely and I long for a family, but just not my own.

I long for a cigarette, but if I enter the house smelling like freshly smoked tobacco, my mother will have a conniption. She's a health nut, regardless of how many bottles of wine reside in the basement. Smoking is entirely prohibited.

My hand wraps around the front door handle as I take in a steadying breath. I won't let myself be affected, I won't rise to any occasion, and I won't let anger dictate my reactions. No matter what they say or how they make me feel, I will remain stoic.

I open the door to the scent of tomato sauce, homemade pasta, basil, garlic, parmesan cheese, and roasting bread. My mouth begins to water as my nostrils flare to suck in the scents.

At least when my mother is home, she has the cook prepare decadent meals, which I refuse to do. I leave them up to their own devices and eat whatever it is they package for me in the fridge. Chicken and roast vegetables, fish and rice, and it never really matters because I don't eat for enjoyment. Most of the time it lays forgotten in the fridge because I'll cook for myself.

I head into the kitchen to find my father sitting at the table reading a newspaper, and my mother standing out on the veranda with her arms crossed over her chest, and her head tipped up toward the sky. Her dyed blonde hair is needing a touch up as her dark brown roots grow in, and then there's my father with his silver hair and matching beard, giving him a distinguished look.

"Hello, son." His voice booms across the kitchen. "I was wondering when you'd come back home."

"Not used to having a full house."

"Then maybe it's time you did something with your life. Surround yourself with people," he snaps. "Instead of staying in this house doing God knows what each damn day."

It's the same lecture over and over again, and I know I should be used to it by now, but it takes everything in me to grit my jaw and keep my mouth shut. I need to stay unaffected.

The door opens as my mother steps in, her dark eyes giving me a quick scan before her mouth tips up at the corners. "Hi, baby."

"Hello, Mother."

"We're about to get started. We're just waiting for your sister."

"Aren't we always?"

"Let's not fight tonight," Mother says as she flicks her hair off her shoulder. "It's been a while since we've all been together. I would like to have a peaceful dinner and catch up on what's been happening recently."

Dad flicks his newspaper and grumbles something under his breath. I can just imagine something along the lines of absolutely nothing has been happening, and I guess he'd be right. I lived a mundane, boring life, up until recently, that is.

I sit at the table to the right of my father and prop my elbow to the wooden surface, resting my chin in my hand. I let loose a long exhale as my stomach grumbles.

"Where is Danielle?" Dad snaps. "It's just a family dinner."

"She's doing it for your attention," I inform him as I move my chin along my hand to face him. "That's why she does most of the shit she does, just to get a reaction out of you."

"Oh, now you know everything there is to know about our family? Why we do the things we do? Is that it?" He drops the newspaper down to the floor. "Tell me, son. Why is it you can't put that same energy into figuring out your life?"

"Stop it," Mother hisses. "Angelo, I said not tonight!" she screams at my father.

"Maria, he just sits here in the house all day, every day, without a purpose. He is my son, but he has no ambition."

"Monty has time to figure it out. We need to concentrate on Danielle's future first."

"You'd probably have a better chance of me finding my ambition," I interject as Dad snorts.

"He's not wrong, Maria."

Mother throws up her hands just as the doorbell rings.

"Who could that be?" she asks. "Did you invite anyone over, Angelo?"

"Absolutely not." My father straightens his tie.

My sister's heels hit the stairs with loud clicking noises as the ringing of the doorbell still reverberates around the house like an echo of ominous energy. My heart begins to pound inside my rib cage, the force of it making my ears grow hot and my skin clammy. It's like my body is trying to prepare me for something my mind hasn't yet caught up with. A premonition of what lies on the other side of my front door.

I begin to stand when I hear the door opening and my sister's shrill voice ringing louder than the doorbell, chiming through my ears like nails on a chalkboard.

"Ford!" she exclaims. "I'm so glad you could make it."

"Did you invite Ford?" my mother asks, her voice sounding garbled and distorted beyond the ringing in my ears.

I slowly shake my head as Danielle's footsteps *click clack* closer toward the kitchen.

I turn just as they step into the room. Ford is in his one good suit with my sister's arm looped in his, and the air escapes my lungs as blood rushes through my face like lava igniting my skin.

He gives me an apologetic look, but all I see is red.

FORD

He looks murderous and completely taken off guard.

There was no time to prepare him. If I came here to warn him I was invited to dinner, I wouldn't have had any time to go home and soak my hands and scrub away the grease that still echoes underneath my nails and on the pads of my fingers.

I didn't want to sit at the dinner table with the Marcatos and look filthy, disheveled, and more out of place than what I already am. But now I'm starting to regret that decision because I don't think I'll make it past dessert with my life intact.

"Ford Rossi." Maria Marcato stands, her arms outstretched as she approaches me. She kisses both of my cheeks before pulling back. "How are you? How's the family?"

"Great." I nod, my eyes still settled on her son who's standing stock still in front of his chair. His body is wound so tight, I fear it's going to snap in half.

"It's great to have you here. Come, sit. Have dinner," Maria says. She guides me to the table, pulling out the chair beside Monty. "Monty, you didn't tell us you invited Ford."

"That's because I didn't," he says through his teeth.

Danielle grabs my arm, leading me to the other side of the table with her. "That's because I did," she states. "Ford helped me with Romeo today."

"Helped you? What? How? What's wrong with the car?" Angelo Marcato finally looks up at his daughter, his blue eyes filled with contempt. "What have you done now?"

"No, Daddy," she leans over and kisses his cheek, "just an oil change."

"Good. I'm glad you're keeping up with that, and you're lucky Ford was available to do it on such short notice."

"Yes, lucky indeed," Monty snarls as he yanks out his chair.

The tension in the room is so thick I could cut it with a knife, but it seems I'm the only one we can sense it as the rest of the Marcatos are oblivious. There will be pain later, I know it.

"I can't stay long, I fear," I tell them as I put a napkin across my lap. "I work at the carnival during the evenings."

"The carnival?" Danielle leans forward, the scent of her perfume clouding around my head. "I would love to go to the carnival."

"He said he works there," Monty reiterates. "He doesn't go there for fun."

"Well, yes," I shrug. "It is work, but it is also fun."

That's when I remember my uniform is upstairs in Monty's room, and the thought of having to go up there to get it before I leave sends my pulse through the roof.

"You need to rub some of that ambition off onto my son," Angelo says as the cook comes to the table and serves the pasta. "It wouldn't hurt him to have a job as well."

I keep my head down to avoid answering Angelo or looking at his son, who's shooting laser beams into my head. I know the longer I avoid him, the worse my punishment will be. The fact that I'm slightly excited more than I'm apprehensive means I'm a masochist. Doesn't it?

I'm lost in the sea of conversation between Danielle and her parents, half listening while eating. I continue to keep my eyes on my plate. Monty has yet to utter a single word, but I can hear his fork snapping off his plate louder than any voice around me.

His anger is palpable, and even though I understand where he's coming from, it's beginning to piss me off. I'm not sure why he would be so angry. I haven't physically done anything with Danielle, and I know I don't stand a chance. Just as well as he knows, I'm the poor boy from the other side of the tracks. I only get to entertain the rich daughters until something suitable comes along.

I drop my fork to my plate and grab the napkin from across my lap to wipe my mouth. "Sorry," I say to everyone. "But I need to get going."

"Thank you for coming." Maria smiles. "It was nice to see you again, Ford."

I finally look at Monty, to find his eyes saturated with rage. "I believe my uniform is in your room."

He shoves back his chair, the loud scraping noise ripping through the silence of the kitchen, then nods for me to follow him.

"Maybe I'll come by and visit you later," Danielle says. "Where do you work at the carnival?"

"Why don't you come by and try to find me?"

She giggles into her napkin, the sound a delicate tinkle. "I would love to."

I nod to Angelo and head out of the kitchen, listening as Monty's feet hit each stair with loud resounding *thuds*. I take my time following behind him, knowing I'm about to enter into a raging storm. Even though it feels calm and quiet right now, I understand it's because I'm standing in the eye of it all.

I get to the top of the stairs and head toward his bedroom, my feet dragging along the carpet runner. I'm not afraid of Monty. I just don't want to disappoint him. He gets enough of that from his family, but I refuse to be treated like a puppet, bending to his will only.

Just as I step inside his bedroom, his hand wraps around my throat, yanking me in farther and slamming me against the wall. I stare into his icy blue eyes as his breath hits my face in heavy pants. His fingers tremble around my throat, and I know it's not from fear or trepidation. It's because he's holding himself back.

"Did you invite my sister to the fucking carnival?"

"Anyone can go to the carnival, Monty." My hand fists into the shirt at his chest. "Stop acting absurd. Have I ever given you a reason not to trust me?"

"I've seen envy cloud your eyes for most of our lives. You've always wanted to be a Marcato, haven't you?"

His words are like sharpened daggers aimed at my ego, and each one hits its target on point.

"You're right." As I release his shirt, I nod. "I have envied you most days. I wish I could stay home, drink bottles of wine, and sit to smoke on a balcony under the Venetian sun. I wish I could walk the streets at night without a single worry, but I never wanted to be a Marcato."

His mouth slams into mine, the kiss holding no semblance of passion. It feels like a punishment, rough and demanding, sharp stings and blood-tinged, but I kiss him back because I can feel the insecurity. Monty has never felt good enough, and in some brutal way, he's trying to prove to me he is.

I'm suddenly released, the back of my head bouncing off the wall with the force of him breaking away, and then my uniform is thrown at my chest. The stupid hat bouncing off my face.

"Get out," he says with his back to me.

If I wasn't so late for work, I'd probably attempt to calm his tumultuous attitude, but I don't have time to cater to Monty, not when I need to make money for my family to survive. I slip out of this room and hurry down the hall, taking the steps at a rapid speed, only to nearly bowl over Danielle at the bottom.

The bells on the hat ring as she looks at it with wide eyes. "You are the jester?"

"And you're a cheat," I tease. "I told you to come and figure it out."

"We can walk there together."

"I'm already running late, I'll have to jog, but you take your time and when you get there, you'll see me."

Her hand runs the length of the buttons on my shirt, her fingers gliding over each one and the pressure increasing the lower she descends. By the time she hits the waistband of my trousers, my cock is pulsing against my zipper. There's no way she can't see it.

It's a dangerous game I'm playing here inside the Marcato mansion. I'm flirting with Danielle, but I tend to fuck her brother. Life doesn't get any more complicated than this.

"I'll see you soon," she husks out. She leans up on her toes to kiss my cheek, dropping her hand from my waistband and letting those long, pointed nails scrape along my erection.

Then she steps back, tossing me a wink, and heads up the stairs. I follow her with my eyes, watching as her tight ass sways with each step, and as she nears the top, my eyes skim to her brother, who's glaring at me. If looks could kill, I'd be dead on the spot.

CHAPTER
EIGHT

MONTY

TWO WEEKS LATER

It's the last night of the carnival, and it's been two weeks since I've laid eyes on Ford. We've never spent this much time apart since the day we first met, and I have no one else to blame but myself. I scared him off with how hot my temper flared and how venomous my jealousy had become.

I gave him his space. I didn't seek him out, and to be honest, it was a much-needed reprieve for me. My insides were becoming so intertwined with his, but I was losing sight of who I was. My reactions to the events that were happening with Danielle and Christina, and just about anybody who looked at him, were borderline insane.

I'm not in love with Ford. At least, I don't think so. I love him like a brother at the moment. The thought leaves my mind and I cringe because the things I did with him aren't something you would do with your brother. Regardless, I love him as a family member. Someone I've grown with, but beyond that, I think our brief relationship was a moment of experimentation.

I just lost myself for a bit.

I'm feeling better. I've made sure to stay away from Danielle, and from my parents who have been home this entire time, probably the longest they've ever stayed home, and I let myself come back down to sanity. I think it's part of the Marcato gene. Everything we touch we must possess, and Ford fought me on that. That's why I found him so intriguing. He never fully gave himself to me and because of that, I became obsessive.

I spray the cologne on my chest and step back to appraise my outfit for the night. All black. Black trousers, black shirt. I want to blend in. I don't want him to see me coming until it's too late because I fear if he's given the chance, he will run and everything we've built since we were seven years old will crumble into dust.

Danielle has been out of the house more than not, and not having to hear her voice helped in my journey. Although, I've heard my parents talking and they're quite excited, hoping that soon she will settle down. I pray the man who is stupid enough to let her hooks sink that deep into him has a heart of iron, because otherwise, Danielle will rip it out of his chest and eat it.

I step out of the house and suck in the fresh air, something I've been lacking for the past few weeks, and with that alone, there's a little pep added to my step. As I head down the cobblestone lane toward the carnival, I put my hands in my pockets. Tonight it will be packed since it's the last night, and everyone will want to get their last fix before it's gone for another year.

I never cared much for the carnival. Even when we were kids, it felt like a forced happy place, over the top of excitement and unrealistic joy. None of those things I ever felt authentically.

I walk past the gates and look straight ahead to find Ford on his podium with his banjo, doing his little dance routine. His hat is jiggling, and his legs are flying out as people laugh, and tonight, just like I suspected, he has an immense crowd around him. It would make no sense to approach him now. Besides, there's one other tent I want to visit before it's gone for a year.

The guard at the door knows me well and nods me through right away. Inside, there's a spicy scent as if someone is burning incense, and the tent is crowded, almost filled from side to side. I once again slip along the edge and head toward the stage. The lighting is again low, adding to the ambiance of what will be happening on stage. I wonder if it'll be the jester again, and if so, how will I feel when I see it?

Smoke begins to rise up out of the machines in front of the stage, and low thrumming music plays, the beat resounding inside my chest, igniting a primal urgency. A woman walks out completely nude, wearing a full lace mask on her face. Her hair is pulled back and hidden beneath a black scarf. Her body is perfect. Ample breasts, perky, and the nipples are the color of dusty rose.

Her stomach is toned, leading down to her pubic area, which is clean of any hair. Her skin glistens with oil and her hands are covered with satin gloves that reach to her elbows.

She kneels at the front of the stage, placing her hands on her knees as she sits back on her feet. Her posture is perfectly straight, making her breasts jut outward, the nipples tightening under our perusal.

The beat of the music picks up as she slowly spreads her knees apart, showing us her most private place, and that too is glistening, just like the oil on her skin. Her gloved fingers reach down and slip in through the folds, making her head tip back, and it's at that moment I wish she didn't have that mask on. I would love to see the arousal on her face.

She begins to rub circles into her hardened clit as I grab my cock from the outside of my pants, trying to stave off the overwhelming need to expose myself in a tent full of strangers. Just as she is starting to tremble, her body right there on the edge of her release, someone else steps out on stage. To my astonishment, it's the jester. His hat is skewed to the side of his head, the bells ringing with each step, and this time, he's not wearing any clothing, but his face is still painted with that mask. The lights drop lower, casting us all in shadows as he lands to his knees behind her and pushes her forward.

Her gloved hands hit the stage as her head hangs down between her shoulders. The jester runs his hand along her spine, his fingers moving meticulously slow. I'm guessing he reaches the crack of her ass as he pauses for all of one second, and then continues. From that point onward, we can't see what he's doing, but it's easy to guess as she begins to jerk forward. The jester's fingers are deep inside her. He pulls his fingers free and slips them up into his mouth, the painted mask looking eerie as he sucks the woman juices from each digit. Then just by the movements alone, I know he's lining himself up. Then he rams inside of her.

There are a few collective gasps around me at the blatant sexual act on stage, but as intoxicating as it is to watch, just watching isn't enough. This is what led me to fuck my best friend a month ago. It's hard to suppress instinctual urges when our most basic instinct is to procreate, and it's right there in front of your face.

The sounds of slapping flesh are all that's coming from the show on the stage. Neither participant makes a sound or says anything, but it's clear she's taking a brutal pounding.

My body is becoming overheated and sweat slides down the back of my neck, slipping down my spine. I'm finding it difficult to drag in a whole lungful of air. My lungs burn with the need to breathe, my heart is speeding as the jester wraps his hands around her waist and really begins to fuck her.

His thrusts fall out of rhythm as the veins along his forearms pop. His chest tightens and the tendons in his neck become prominent. The pure euphoria emanating from the both of them is intoxicating, even though I can't see either of their features. But I am able to imagine myself in his place, my cock sliding in and out of her, my hips slapping off her ass and reddening the skin.

Her arms are shaking as she's in the deep throes of her orgasmic release. Her breasts are swinging with each heaving breath, and with shock I watch as the jester reaches around to grab the mask on her face, crumbling it in his hand and ripping it away.

My mind scrambles to keep pace with the vision in front of me, but everything zones out and my vision begins to darken. My body ripples with goosebumps and the sweat dries ice cold on my skin in an instant. I stagger backward as disbelief courses through me, as every hair on the surface of my body stands on end.

It can't be.

But there it is in front of my face, as plain as day. I can't fight reality and what's plainly there in front of me, no matter how hard I try.

I find the flap of the tent and make it outside just as the bile rushes up from my stomach and spews from my mouth, disgust amplified within me at my reaction to being naïve.

I just envisioned myself wanting to fuck my own sister.

I finally straighten and instead of going back into that tent and demanding my sister follow me out, I decide to forget this even happened. The embarrassment would be too overwhelming. Then the sound of laughter hits me like a tidal wave, and I focus my sights on the jester I know acting like an idiot on the podium. My rage is back tenfold. If it weren't for him, Danielle wouldn't have come to this carnival, and like me, maybe she stumbled upon that tent and the lure was too much for her to ignore.

Danielle has always been swayed by the darker side of life, so as much as I'm disgusted, I'm not fucking surprised.

My feet take me straight to the idiot on the podium, each stomp of my heel like a crack of thunder before an impending storm. I reach the platform and grab the back of his uniform, yanking him hard to the ground. His ass meets the dirt with a loud whoosh and before he can react, I have his uniform fisted in my hand and I'm yanking him up to my face.

"Do you fucking know what my sister is doing here?"

He struggles, trying to yank my hand away from his uniform, his fingers wrapping around my wrist.

I give him a shake and snarl, "Answer me, you coward."

His nails bite into my skin, and I stare down at them. I grit my jaw, and for the second time tonight, I'm rendered speechless. These nails are pristine, clean as a whistle.

"Get the fuck off me, man!" he yells as I look down into his light hazel eyes.

I release him and stumble backward, my heart feeling like it's about to explode as I receive shocking revelation after shocking revelation. This jester is not Ford, which can only mean one thing.

My head slowly turns to look back at the tent as my mouth dries with realization.

I rip the jester hat off his head and crumple it in my fist as I storm toward the exit of the carnival. I'll let this serve as a reminder that even the people you consider being the closest to you, the ones you would trust with anything, can betray you. I'll keep this as a reminder to trust no one again.

Ford was fucking Danielle.

FORD

This is the longest Monty, and I have spent apart. We've been inseparable since we were seven years old, and the fact that he's stayed away from me for two weeks without returning calls has left me questioning our friendship to begin with. Maybe I was nothing but an experiment or a poor toy to play with until his next obsession came along.

Last night was the last night of the carnival, and I'm obviously going to miss the money, given the position I accepted. The pay was more than accommodating, and I think that's also adding a bit to my depressive state. My best friend is MIA, the carnival is over, and I fucked his sister in front of an audience.

Not that he knows that last part.

"Ford!" my mother calls out from downstairs. "We have guests! Please come down."

I'm tired. I don't have any energy to entertain or pretend like I'm not in a foul mood, but I've never been able to let my parents down. Even if it's at my own expense.

I head into the kitchen and stop short when I see Angelo and Maria Marcato sitting at our small aluminum table, its rickety legs uneven. Their pristine clean shoes touching our cracked linoleum tiled floor has shame washing over me for the conditions my family lives in compared to the mansion they live in.

"Come sit down, son." My father pulls out a broken wooden chair, completely mismatched, just like the others. "The Marcatos have something they would like to discuss with you."

I can see Maria's eyes scanning over the kitchen cabinets, and it takes all my willpower not to cringe at the sight she's seeing. Broken cabinet doors, some fully missing. Broken laminate countertops and a dripping, leaky sink.

"Ford, we know how good of a friend you've been to Monty," Angelo begins, and my stomach flips as anxiety bubbles up into my throat, making it hard to breathe. What exactly is this about?

"Yes." My voice shakes, and I inwardly curse myself for sounding like a coward.

"You've been an excellent influence on him and you're a hard worker," Angelo continues. "Something I've been trying to persuade him to do, but I am not here to talk about Monty."

The relief is immediate. I never want anyone to find out what Monty and I did for two weeks this past summer because it didn't mean anything more than two friends who were experimenting. If my parents found out, it would ruin their lives.

"What are you here to talk about?" I clasp my hands together in my lap and try to be patient, but I know Angelo is a talker.

"You've been pretty much our family since you followed Monty home all those years ago. But, son, we would like to make it official."

"Make it official?" I look around the table from Angelo to Maria, who are both smiling with glee, to my mother and then my father, who both look like they're about to pass out with happiness. Are they giving me up for adoption?

"Danielle has spoken of her affection for you, saying how she feels about you is different from how she's ever felt about anyone else," Maria says, her eyes shining with unshed tears. "We think you would be a great husband for her."

"Husband?"

My ears ring as my vision tunnels, sounds around me becoming distorted as if underwater. The Marcatos want to marry me into their family.

"You would be a Marcato, though. You would have to give up your last name. I've spoken to your parents, and I've promised to make it worth their while since you are their only son."

"I would no longer be a Rossi?" My stomach stinks with the realization that I would be giving up my identity in the name of wealth and power. Even though for many years I had hoped the Marcatos would adopt me, that I would have taken their name in a heartbeat, now that I'm faced with it, the only thing stirring inside of me is grief.

Angelo pushes a file toward me, making this feel more like a business transaction than a love arrangement. "Your parents have agreed. We will buy them a new home, make sure they can retire in peace while you become the very best husband for our Danielle."

"You haven't said much, Ford." Maria's head tips to the side. "Is this not what you want?"

I guess to them, wealth is something everyone strives for, and in a way, yes, I work day in and day out, hoping to one day make enough money to survive. But this situation isn't just about Danielle and me. I also have to consider Monty, regardless of if he no longer wants to be my friend. I don't think he'll appreciate his onetime lover marrying his sister, especially for wealth and power.

"How does Monty feel about this?" I ask.

"We have not spoken to Monty about it," Angelo informs me. "Soon we'll be finding him a wife and his days of lounging around the house will be done. I will put him to work."

"I will be honest with you guys," I place my hands on the table, linking my fingers together, "Monty will not like this situation, and if I agree to it, I will be agreeing to a new wife in exchange for losing my best friend. That very best friend who introduced me to you, who I've hung out with almost every day since we were seven years old. It would be deceiving."

"Don't you want a better life for your parents?" Maria asks, hitting the most vulnerable point. "Monty's anger is quick and burns hot, but it will fade overtime. Will you say no to your best chance at a comfortable life for your family just because of my son's temper tantrums?"

"I don't understand why Monty would be mad." Angelo shrugs. "His best friend would become his brother."

There's nothing I can say about that. I can't explain to them that my best friend, who was also my lover, would hate that I became his brother. Not to mention, the rivalry between Danielle and him would only increase, and she would use me, as her husband, to always choose her side. Monty would have no one. But Maria is right. For my whole life, my parents have always thought of me, put me before themselves, and now I have the opportunity to do that. What kind of son would I be if I didn't jump at the chance to give them the life they deserve?

I open the folder and stare down at the very legal-looking document. Everything is laid out in ink. I will marry Danielle Marcato, forfeiting my family name in the process. We are to stay married or everything in this agreement becomes void. My parents will not receive a new home until the marriage is complete. They will not be provided for until I've looked at their daughter and said I do.

A pen appears on top of the paper, the gold surface engraved with the Marcato name. "Sign it, son," Angelo says.

My fingers tremble as I pick up the pen. The small object feels like it weighs over one hundred pounds. I grip it between my fingers, the icy surface quickly seeping into the skin and sending an ominous chill through my bones, but with the shaky hand, I sign my signature along the dotted line. Probably the last time I'll ever sign it as a Ford Rossi.

I hand the pen back to Angelo, close up the file, and handing that over to him as well. As my parents and Monty's parents celebrate with excited chatter about the future, and the size of the wedding, I sit quietly in my seat as a dark premonition washes over me.

Inviting Danielle to the carnival was my gravest mistake because, just like Monty, she found me easily that night. Only I wasn't in the same position as before. I was still a jester, but my role was meant for a smaller crowd.

I should have known she would stumble upon that tent because Danielle oozes sex. So, of course, she's also attracted to it. She volunteered to be a part of the show after that, and that's when she and I found ourselves becoming carnally inter-twined. I will admit, I enjoy fucking Danielle Marcato, and if there's nothing else, at least I can look forward to that.

The Marcatos get up to leave, shaking all of our hands just like a proper business deal, and as my father walks them out. My mother sits there and heavily scrutinizes me. To her, I'm an open book, she can read just about anything in every facial expression, my body language, all of it. There's not much I can hide from her.

"Why are you not happy?" she asks.

"I am happy for our family," I tell her.

"I know you are happy for the family." She reaches out to grab my hand. "I know how much you would do for this family, but the Marcatos are like your second family. I thought you would be more excited than this."

"Danielle will not be an easy wife," I tell her. "She's impulsive and fickle, and most of all,

Monty will not accept it. Our friendship will be over."

"Oh, son. I truly believe Maria was telling the truth. I think Monty will get over it and then he will be so happy to actually have you as a loyal brother."

Of course, she doesn't know the extent Monty and I went to in exploring our friendship, and no one knows how well he can hold a grudge like I do. I truly believe our time together had him somehow claiming ownership over me. The feeling of being possessed by him was at first intoxicating, but gradually became annoying.

I have to believe that maybe he'll be mad until the day he finds his own wife, then he'll finally realize that everything we did was just something new and exciting to pass the time.

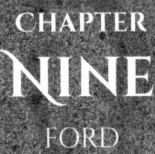

I arrived at the garage the next day, seeing it in a different light. The Marcatos want me to quit and become a stay-at-home husband to their daughter, because now that she doesn't have the discipline of school to keep her in line, they're worried she'll get herself into unsavory situations.

Too bad she's already done that and with me.

I have no other choice but to agree because I signed a contract, and the more I think about it, the more I realize I just signed my life over. No longer will I be able to make decisions without consulting the Marcatos, and even though I said I would do anything for my family, sacrifice anything so that they could live comfortably, I don't think I actually meant it.

I'd rather work three jobs and hand over every bit of my paycheck to my parents instead of becoming a toy to the family I once considered my own.

There's no going back now.

I'm just about to open the door to the garage when a hand fists the back of my coveralls and pulls me to the side of the building. I struggle, but when I turn and find Monty, all thought processes leave my mind.

"You finally did it." His back falls against the brick wall as he pulls a cigarette out from the pack in his pocket, taking his sweet time to light it. "You finally pulled off your life's ambition," he finishes on his smoke's exhale.

"Your parents seemed to think you would be happy with it, that we would finally be brothers." I cross my arms over my chest, not liking the way my heart picks up at the sight of him.

He's wearing all black again, the trousers molding to his legs, and then a silk button-up top showing an enormous expanse of his chest. His hair is combed back, shining slick under the sun, and those blue eyes are staring at me with calculating precision.

"And you believed them?" His laugh is sarcastic as he takes another hit on his smoke. "I knew you would one day marry, Ford. I'm not an idiot, but my sister? Why my sister? Are you punishing me?"

"Have you spoken to Danielle?" I ask. "You have to know this was not my idea."

"Why would I speak to Danielle? I'm coming to my best friend, the one person I thought gave a shit about mc. Why her?"

"She initiated it, and your parents were happy about it. My parents are ecstatic because their son is going to be a part of a family he considered to be his own since he was a child, and yes, it was an opportunity I couldn't pass up. What your parents are offering to do for mine is something I wouldn't have been able to achieve in this lifetime. No matter how many jobs I work."

"Maybe if the carnival was here all year round. You were working so hard there and making good money. Weren't you?"

His question has an undertone of accusation. I can hear it. He can't know exactly what I was doing at the carnival. He would have called me out on it for sure. That's not something Monty would be able to keep to himself.

"Even so." I shrug. "I still wouldn't be able to match what your parents are offering."

"So it's a business transaction." He flicks his cigarette to the ground, smoke still rising from the red cherry at the tip.

My eyes zero in on the hot coal and suddenly this is feeling more like an interrogation. It just hasn't become violent yet.

"Yes," I admit. "It is more like a business transaction. You know I don't feel for Danielle the way a husband should."

"Does she know that?" He turns so his shoulder rests on the brick as he faces me, those cold eyes sending shards of ice to my heart.

"I would assume so. I've never told her differently. At least that's the truth."

With a nod, he pushes himself off the wall. "I will give you this warning once, and I implore you to really think this over before the day comes. Danielle is like a sponge, she will suck everything in that's around her until she's filled to capacity, and then you'll think you'll have a reprieve, that she's changed, but it's only until she's depleted, and then the cycle starts again. She will change you and you will begin to hate this life."

I don't bother to disagree with him because I don't know what Danielle is capable of, and I know as her husband, I'll be her target for most of our lives.

He chuckles, taking my silence as if he has rendered me speechless. As if I'm surprised by what his sister is capable of. "There's still time to get out of this." His fingertips lift my chin upward, and my heart begins to pound. "Does she get this reaction from you?" he whispers as his finger glides down over my jugular. No doubt feeling the rapid beat of my pulse. "Does she make your skin break out in goosebumps, while your heart feels like it's going to skip right out of your chest?" That finger continues to glide over my chest and down over my sternum. "Does she give you a desire so great that you would fuck her behind a tent?" His hand wraps around my cock, which, of course, is hard and pulsing.

I swallow down the lump in my throat as my eyes begin to burn, because I can see it as clear as day shining through Monty's eyes. He's not jealous, he's not obsessed. None of those things are pouring out in this moment of unguarded emotions. Monty Marcato is in love with me.

I'm stunned as I stare back into his eyes, and when I stay silent, he releases me and blinks once again, putting up his wall of indifference. This thing between us has gone too far and now I fear there's no coming back from it, not without breaking his heart. I do not share the same feelings he does. I have never been in love, and now with my current predicament, I may never be in love.

"So, I'm the best man, right?" He holds out his hands, somehow putting a smile on his mouth even though it doesn't quite reach his eyes. "I have to plan the bachelor party."

"You don't have to do that."

"I'm your best friend, Ford. Or has that changed, too?"

I want to tell him that yes, it has changed. That we've barely spoken to each other in almost three weeks, that the moment we fell into bed together, it destroyed our friendship, even more so now that he's in love with me.

"A bachelor party, huh?" I swallow down the fear working its way up inside of me, and I try my best to look to the future and ignore the warning bells that are going off inside my head.

"Do you think Christina or Diana would want to come by?" He throws me a wink. "Maybe they could do a few dances." He begins to sway his hips as a chuckle worms its way out of my throat.

"I have a feeling they would want nothing to do with us now." I shake my head.

"Speak for yourself." He gives me a taunting smile, the look raising all the hair along my arms. This wouldn't be Monty if he didn't have some form of revenge ready, and if that means he wants to pursue my ex-girlfriend in retaliation, then I won't hold him back from that.

"I wish you luck then." I scratch at the scruff on my face. "You are probably a better match in her parents' eyes, anyway."

His face falls with my confession, and he leans in to press his forehead to mine. I smell a hint of nicotine and his cologne, dragging me back in time to three weeks ago when we were so engrossed in each other. His eyes are sealed shut, his face a mask of agony, and usually my job as his best friend would be to pull him out of it, to save him from his own dark feelings. But I can't be that person anymore.

"Kiss me," he whispers. "One last time. I will never speak about what happened between us ever again."

I want to refuse him because I fear kissing him will only fuel his hope for us, but maybe there's a chance he needs closure. Something neither of us were given, because if Danielle hadn't come home when she did, I could say with the utmost certainty that Monty and I would still be fucking each other.

So I grab the sides of his face, letting the tips of my fingers glide under his ears as I guide his mouth toward mine. His lips tremble as I press mine into them, as if he's nervous or holding himself back, but just as I'm about to pull away, his mouth opens and seals over mine, sucking my bottom lip into his mouth and dragging the flesh with his teeth.

I pull away and take a step back as he laughs, his fingers running along his glistening mouth. I can only hope that gives him the closure he needs, and maybe we can go back to being best friends. Now that I'm marrying Danielle, we can be brothers.

"I have a bachelor party to plan." He snaps his fingers as he steps around me. "I'll reach out."

"We have time." I turn and watch his retreating back, his shoulders shaking with laughter.

"The wedding is in two weeks," he calls over his shoulders.

And suddenly I feel like I've been doused in ice-cold water. I didn't look at the date of the wedding on the contract.

MONTY

His taste still lingers on my lips as I walk home. For a moment there, I let my guard down, hoping he would see exactly how I'm feeling and turn this whole thing around. Since the night I found him in the tent fucking my sister, I've come to the realization that maybe the person I thought Ford was happened to be only a figment of my imagination. Or maybe the relationship we had developed so briefly this summer was all a figment of my imagination.

It's time I let it go, especially since I laid it all out, baring myself to him, and he locked up tighter, sealing everything he could away. Marrying my sister may not have been his life's goal, but the perks of such a marriage were his life's goal, and I doubt he would drop all of that for me.

So I begged him to kiss me just so I could taste him and his ultimate rejection, because I can't live with this hatred inside of me much longer. I either have to accept everything or I do something extreme and ruin our families' lives.

I might be impulsive, and certainly lacking empathy, but I'm not here to ruin lives, so I'll learn to accept it. Now, I have a bachelor party to plan. That's what the best man does. He plans a night of complete debauchery as the groom bids farewell to his freedom, and it's fitting really because Ford will never be free again, he'll know exactly what it means to be a Marcato.

I think it's stupid he didn't read the fucking contract, that he didn't know his own wedding is in two weeks. He was probably just staring at all the dollar signs, not really caring what he was sacrificing in exchange, but he will know. He'll learn the hard way, and as his best friend, I think it's only right if I'm there to help him through it.

I head up my driveway just as my sister pulls in and parks her car. The door opens, and her six-inch heel hits the stone, her long, bare leg shining as the sunlight reflects off of the cream she has smothered onto her skin. I'm suddenly trans-ported back to that tent as bile begins to rush up my throat.

Her head appears, her caramel- highlighted hair blowing in the breeze as she turns her head and finds me standing there, looking at her as nausea swirls through my stomach.

"Little brother," she coos. "Be a doll and help me take these bags into the house?"

I ignore her and walk by, letting my shoes echo off the stone with each step. I'll never lift a finger for the bitch again.

"I know you're jealous," she calls out. "I'm not stupid. I know there was something there between you and Ford, but you must know, it would never be accepted."

Her words send a chill down my spine just as I hit the front door. I don't open it, but I don't turn to look at her either.

"Father would kill you; Mother would be devastated. Did you really want all of that to happen?"

So in her mind, she's a martyr. She saved me from being gay with my best friend by marrying him herself. I guess I should be thankful, right? What sister would do that for her brother?

"Do you think I actually want him?" she continues. "I haven't even kissed him yet."

That may be the truth because there wasn't a whole lot of kissing in that tent that night, even so, her words are beginning to run too close together in a quick rapid-fire succession. As if she's confessing to something and hoping for my acceptance, but I know it's nothing but a sham.

Everything Danielle does is for her gain only.

So, with a slight shrug of my shoulders, I open the door and disappear into the house. I'm no longer worried about my summer tryst with Ford and my parents finding out. So if she thinks she can hold that over my head, she's dead wrong. I've lost everything, and do you know what they say about a man who's lost everything? He has nothing more to lose.

"Monty!" my mother calls from the kitchen when she hears the door shut. "Is that you?"

I don't feel like answering her either, so I start up the stairs, but she doesn't let it go that easily.

"Hey, you didn't hear me calling you?" she asks from right behind me, and I turn around to look at her.

"What do you want?"

"We're going to need help with the wedding preparations. I need you to start getting fitted for your tux and maybe you can take Ford to our tailor and have the suits picked out together. Your sister wants to do cream."

"Cream," I laugh. "Sure, whatever."

My sister comes inside the house, huffing and puffing, her hands filled with bags. "Mother, please help me take these."

I exhale a sigh of relief and head up the stairs, just as I'm hearing my mother gasp and my sister squeal behind me.

"Isn't it so sexy?" Danielle exclaims. "I think he's going to love it for our wedding night."

Their wedding night. She must be talking about sexy lingerie, trying to convince my mother it'll be the first time she's been fucked, and by Ford. Which neither of that is true. So, with a loud sarcastic chuckle, I get to the top of the stairs and head toward my bedroom.

I step out onto the balcony, resting my hands on the stone balustrade, and look up at the Venetian sky. I wish I could turn back time to two months ago when my best friend stood down on the street and begged me to go for a gondola ride. There are so many things I would do differently, but not even all the money in the world can turn back time, and we all have to live with the consequences of our decisions.

I light a smoke and sit on the chair, mentally going over the things I need to do to prepare for an epic bachelor party, one that will go down as the most prolific night of Ford's life. Even over-shadowing his wedding night.

My eyes skip to the jester's hat that's sitting on my dresser, and that small part of me that doesn't want to let go begins to reminisce the way the bells sounded as I thrusted into him that night at the carnival. How his nails tried to find purchase on the wooden crate as I took him for the first time.

My cock hardens with the memory, but I leave it as it is because I refused to give in to the weakness that's always been Ford.

Maybe we'll have a carnival themed bachelor party.

CHAPTER
TEN
FORD

The Marcato mansion is lit up like a carnival. There are neon lights around the windows, what looks to be a tent in the backyard, and that eerie tinkling music. I hate to admit I've missed all of it. Monty really did go all out.

When I walk in through the front door, a lot of acquaintances that we've known over the years are standing around. Guys from the garage and a few other guys who worked at the carnival all greet me. There are fried foods and cotton candy, and when I walk into the kitchen I find Monty standing there with a jester hat on his head.

"Where did you get that hat?" I ask him with a laugh.

"I can't tell you my ways," he snickers.

"Thanks for doing this." I'm sincere in my gratitude because for the past two weeks, I've been struggling with dark foreboding thoughts. Nightmares have plagued my sleep, images of darkened rooms, damp scents, and being trapped. When I expressed my fears to my mother, she said it was normal and my nightmares were just cold feet.

So being here with my best friend, having a party, finally lightens up the whole situation. I'm not nervous or have cold feet about marrying Danielle. I've come to accept that. I think mostly I'm worried about losing my best friend, or finally disappointing my parents.

"Hey, look what I got." Monty breaks through my thoughts and holds up a bottle of amontillado.

My stomach flips at the sight of the dark liquid, but I laugh and pick up a glass from the counter. "Let's do it."

His eyes shine with mirth as he sets the bottle back down. "First, let's just start with some normal wine. I remember what amontillado does to your stomach on its own."

He fills up both of our glasses with a white wine and motions for me to follow him out into the backyard.

"Where are your parents?"

"Staying with my sister at the hotel where you two will be married tomorrow."

I down my glass of wine in one gulp at the mention of my wedding tomorrow. I don't really want to talk about it tonight, even though this is what the party is for. I kind of just want to be with my best friend.

"I wish we could go ride gondolas," I admit to him.

I watch as his throat works, swallowing down his glass of wine, and then he finally turns to look at me, a sad look in his bright blue eyes. "Me too, Ford."

Within no time, we finish off the first bottle of wine, and more people have gravitated out to the backyard to smoke and to laugh. I just keep staring at the tent, wondering why we haven't gone inside.

"What's in the tent?" I point out.

"It's just for show." Monty shrugs. "Do you like it?"

"Yeah, how did you find the same pattern as the tents at the carnival?"

"My ways, Ford." He wags his finger at me. "Just because you're coming into some money doesn't mean you get to learn my ways."

His arrogant behavior is back, and we're speaking as if the last two months didn't happen. My heart soars because just maybe we can salvage our friendship after all.

After another bottle of white wine, I'm beginning to feel weightless, like all the worry I had weighing down on my shoulders for the past month has suddenly lifted. Lightning skates across the sky, forcing everyone to migrate back inside, but Monty stands there, his feet in the grass and his head tipped up to look at the sky. I start to pray for the rain. I step down from the porch and stand beside him, tipping my head back just as a large raindrop hits my cheek.

"Did you want to go inside the tent?" He holds up the bottle of amontillado and the bells on that silly hat ring with his movements.

"When did you get that?"

"I had someone bring it out for me." He gives me a wink. "Why? Are you scared to drink it?"

"I'm not scared." My chin lifts. "I am a wine connoisseur."

"That's true." He nods as he chuckles, then leads me toward the tent, pulling the flap aside and waving for me to go forward.

As soon as I step in, I know exactly what this is. The stage near the back, the ambient lighting, and even the way the heavy raindrops hit the tent's fabric, reminds me of that low steady beating drum, nearly transporting me back to that carnival.

The heat of his body meets my back as his lips skim over the shell of my ear. "I stumbled upon the tent the first night you were working at the carnival, but truly you were on that podium that night. So tell me, when did you begin working the tent?"

"The third day," I answer him honestly. "The pay doubled."

"Always the money." He chuckles. "There is no need for morals when there are a few extra zeros on a paycheck. Am I right?"

The words he's saying are mean, but they're not sad and angry. It's more curiosity, so I decide to answer him truthfully. "Money has been the single most important thing to me since I realized my family is poor," I admit to him.

His hand comes around to rest on my stomach, slowly gathering my shirt into his palm and exposing the skin. His fingertips glide across the surface, and I'm feeling many things at once. Lust, desire, fear, apprehension, but most of all, I don't want to let him down.

"Why don't you take these off?" He tugs on my shirt. "What do you say to one last time? Before you marry my sister and become my brother for real."

I could say no, and I could leave this place, but his hand is already wrapped around my hard cock, squeezing it through the material of my pants. No matter how much this man pisses me off, he can still pull a reaction from me, and he has the evidence of that in his palm.

So I pull my shirt over my head and begin to undo my pants, letting them drop to a pool at my feet. I slowly slip out of my shoes and turn toward him.

He grabs my shoulder and steers me toward the stage. "Up there," he demands.

I have no problems performing on stage. I've done it many times. So my steps are sure and even as I approach the platform and step up onto the wood surface.

"On all fours," he tells me as his shirt drops next to mine. There's a sad look in his eye, like he knows this is the last time we'll ever get a chance to be together, and that's my fault too, because of the decisions I made.

He steps up and behind me, dropping that same small tube of lube the tent was giving out at the carnival, and he rips open the condom with his teeth, the foil crinkling. Then he's pushing me down by my shoulders, putting me in the perfect position, and that's when I realize things are moving so fast. There would be no stopping it right now, even if that's what I wanted.

My ass is smeared with lube, and then my best friend is pushing inside of me, and for the first time in over a month, I feel like I'm home. He's gentle with me, and this is nothing like our lust-filled fucks in the past. Monty is making love to me.

His hands come down over my back, grabbing into the globes of my ass as his thrusts slow, and I'm shocked when my tears hit the wooden planks in front of me.

"I love you, Ford," Monty admits. "And I know you love me too, so I promise you I will treasure our love and seal it away forever."

I don't know if it's the alcohol coursing through me or the fact that we're doing this again, and maybe deep down, I'd hope we would, but I'm beginning to regret agreeing to marry Monty's sister. This is his final farewell to me. I can feel it, and I don't think our friendship can withstand another farewell.

He groans long and deep as his cock jerks inside of me, and everything is over faster than it began. He pulls out, discards the condom, cleans everything, and then motions for me to put my clothes back on with him. We dress in silence, but I can still feel him there inside of me, and maybe that's what he wanted me to feel tomorrow when I'm marrying his sister.

He holds up the bottle of amontillado as a warm smile creeps along his satisfied face. "Are we ready now?"

"Yeah," I chuckle, knowing this is our last night.

"It's only half a bottle." He shrugs. "We'll have to go get another one later."

"Hell no," I shake my head. "I'm not going into that basement."

He pours us each a glass and then looks up at me through his lashes, his face filled with mischief. "Do you remember that first night we drank this, and we made a deal?"

My stomach sinks as I groan into my fist. "You're calling in your favor now?"

"I don't know a better time. I'm going to need you to come down to the basement and help me bring up more bottles of amontillado."

I down the glass in one gulp, the sound of Monty's laugh ringing inside the tent. I'm going to need as much liquid courage as I can get.

MONTY

His words begin to slur just slightly enough for my sensitive ears to detect. He polished off the half a bottle of amontillado and didn't even notice I hadn't taken a sip out of my glass.

"Are you ready to go to the basement?" I give him a salacious grin as I pop the jester hat back on my head.

"Hell yeah, let's go." He stands from the platform, the same one I just fucked him on and brought him to tears. He stumbles, then rights himself as he heads toward the flap.

I follow behind him out into the night air. The rain has stopped and there's now a cooling breeze. I soak it in, letting it calm my heated skin.

"Let's go. Are you afraid?" He taunts me, and I laugh at his false bravado.

"Maybe a little," I admit.

His eyes softened because he knows I'm not talking about the basement. He figures it's about the wedding and losing him to my sister, but what I'm feeling goes much deeper than that.

When we get inside, we notice mostly everyone has gone home, save for a few passed out bodies on my couch and floor. We ignore the snoring as he leads us to the basement, and then he stops with his hand resting on the door handle.

"Do we really need another bottle?" His voice shakes, and I wonder if he's feeling a premonition. Could he truly know what's waiting for him in those basement catacombs?

"You owe me," I remind him.

Ford pulls open the door to expose the concrete stairs, and down below the dim yellow light flickers with the dampness of the ceiling and walls. I watch his throat work as he swallows down the fear I can see shining bright in his eyes, and then he takes a step, wobbles a bit on his feet but continues.

When we both reach the bottom, he has one hand against the wall, his chest laboring with his breathing, while the other hand is pressed to his forehead. "I feel funny."

"It's 'cause you can't handle all the wine," I tease him.

"No," he shakes his head and falls against the wall, "something's wrong."

I grab him by the arm and pull it around my neck, then begin to haul his dragging feet deeper into the catacombs. "I roofied you."

His head lolls forward as the sound close to a moan escapes his lips. "Mo-Mon-ty."

"You have to understand one thing, Ford." I set him down inside an alcove, pressing his back to the stone wall, watching as his eyes try to focus on my face. "No one attacks me with impunity."

I don't expect an answer as his head rolls back and forth, so I remove the hat from my head, crunching the satin material in my fist, and grinding my molars to stave off the rage. Drool slips from the corner of his mouth as his body completely goes slack.

"You fucked my sister behind my back, then decided it was a good idea to marry into the Marcato wealth. I bet you thought yourself worthy, didn't you? Probably laughed about Monty's poor feelings and his heart, when the whole time you had a plan. Well, Ford, I had one too."

I slip the hat down over his head and grab a small sewing kit I found in the drawer upstairs. I choose a yellow thread, wanting the color to be as bright as possible, and I begin to stitch the fabric into his skin.

The only assurance I have that he's still alive is the few grunts I get when the needle slips through his flesh like butter. Blood drips down his face in thin red rivulets, almost like he's crying tears of crimson.

By the time I'm finished, he's completely passed out, his body hunched over and his hat nearly meeting the filthy floor. This next part may take me all night, but I refuse to back down now that I've come this far. So I open up the tub of mortar and slap a thick line along the ground, then I begin to place my bricks. One after the other in a straight perfect line, and then it's another layer of mortar.

By the time I'm at the second last level of bricks, I hear the bells jingle. "Ford?"

At first it's silent. The bells stop, and I wonder if I gave him too much, until a chuckle escapes through the small hole above my head, and my heart stalls in my chest.

Another layer of mortar and I grab three bricks, placing them on the row, leaving just the smallest hole at the top.

"I refuse to share you with anyone, Ford. Instead, I'm going to seal you away and preserve our love forever." When I slip the last brick in the hole, the bells slowly fade, and I know the real work will now begin.

After a quick shower, I dress in the cream suit I had tailored for my sister's glamorous wedding to my best friend. I gel back my hair and make sure I've dugout every bit of mortar from under my nails.

The hotel is brimming with people, and I first see Ford's parents standing anxiously outside the entrance.

"Oh, Monty!" his mother calls and runs forward. "Have you seen Ford?"

"He went home last night," I tell her as I narrow my eyes. "Are you telling me he's not here?"

"He didn't come home," his father admits. "We cannot find him."

My parents step out at that moment, their faces a mask of irritation. "Where is Ford?" my mother demands.

I hold out my hands and set my jaw. "Looks like he skipped out on the wedding." I brush past them all and step inside the hotel, heading directly for the room I know my sister will be sitting in. She'll be preparing herself for what she believes will be the wedding of the century. I can't wait to be the one to tell her differently.

Danielle turns in her seat when she hears the door opening, her face falling when she sees it's me. "What do you want, little brother?"

"Might as well pack it on up, big sister," I tell her. "It looks like your husband won't be here today."

"What?" She looks at me, her eyes widening beneath her fake lashes.

"Did you really think he'd want to marry you in some arranged situation? Ford is a romantic. He has run off. We'll probably never see him again, and it's all your fault." I turn and walk back out of the room, closing the door on her soft cries, and then I leave the hotel as everyone is in a frantic state trying to look for Ford.

But only I know where he is.

EPILOGUE

The wall is still holding strong, only slight cracks showing in the mortar after all these years. I rest my hand against the bricks and swear they radiate with a warmth of my long-lost friend's love.

People searched for him for months after his disappearance, but with no proof or a trace of his whereabouts, the authorities had to assume he ran away from a life he didn't want. It didn't help when an anonymous caller let them know about his deviant ways at the carnival. Of course, he didn't want to settle down.

"Monty!" Christina calls from upstairs. "Are you bringing the wine?"

I married Christina in a lavish wedding a year after his disappearance, and we are now proud parents of three children. Two boys and a girl. Monty Jr, Ford, and Isabela.

As for Danielle, she never really did recover from Ford's betrayal, and moved back to Paris, never to be heard from again. Hopefully, she's found peace.

Or died.

Neither matters to me.

My parents are traveling the world, and my father is proud of how well I stepped into the role of taking over our family's business.

Life has been good for me, and I attribute it all to the man sealed away in my basement. He's watching over me and my family, and I swear, some nights when I am smoking on my balcony, I can hear those bells ringing.

Also by C.A. Rene

The Whitsborough Chronicles

Through the Pain

Into Darkness

Finding the Light

To Redemption

The Whitsborough Progenies

Ivy's Venom

Carmelo's Malice

Saxon's Distortion

Gabriel's Deception

Desecrated Duet

Desecrated Flesh

Desecrated Essence

The Reaped Series

The Reaper Incarnate

Hunting the Reaper

Claiming the Reaper

Hail Mary Duet

Blue 42

Red Zone

Sacrificial Lambs

Sing Me a Song

Song of Tenebrae

A Verse for Caelum

Steel Dragons MC

Dragon Slayer

Mimic

About the Author

Check out my website www.careneauthor.com for all updates.

The computer screen is my canvas, and the keyboard is my brush. Thank you for viewing my masterpieces. My addictions include coffee, books, and WINE, in that order.

Please join my FB Group and show the love! I appreciate it!

C.A.'S Renegades

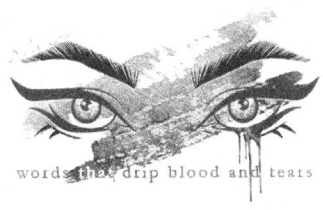

www.ingramcontent.com/pod-product-compliance
Lightning Source LLC
Chambersburg PA
CBHW061232170626
46809CB00007B/2640